Once again, Grace's eyes were drawn to the baby

Emily was kicking her feet, her attention captured by some reflection in the window. She'd filled out since her birth, and now, at six weeks, she weighed over ten pounds. A perfect baby, Grace thought. The kind of baby anyone would want…

Maybe I should place her for adoption. Wouldn't that be the best thing for her? To have two parents who really want a baby? I'm sure I wouldn't have any problem doing it once the court knew her mother had abandoned her….

Grace reached over and touched Emily's hand. The baby immediately latched on to her forefinger, and then, in a stunning moment Grace knew she'd never forget, Emily smiled. It was her first real smile.

At that moment Grace's heart contracted, love filling her. "I'll do my very best for you, sweetheart," she promised. "Whatever it takes, I won't let you down."

Patricia Kay

Patricia Kay is a *USA TODAY* bestselling author whose
first mainstream novel was nominated for a RITA® Award
by the Romance Writers of America. She has written
more than forty-five novels over the past sixteen years,
both romance and women's fiction. She and her husband
live in Houston, Texas, and have three children and three
grandchildren. To learn more about her, she invites you to
visit her Web site at www.patriciakay.com.

Patricia Kay
Which End
Is Up?

WHICH END IS UP?

Copyright © 2006 by Patricia A. Kay

isbn-13:978-0-373-88111-6

isbn-10:   0-373-88111-8

This edition published by arrangement with Harlequin Books S.A.

® and TM are trademarks of the publisher. Trademarks indicated with
® are registered in the United States Patent and Trademark Office, the
Canadian Trade Marks Office and in other countries.

TheNextNovel.com

 HARLEQUIN®

PRINTED IN U.S.A.

From the Author

Dear Reader,

Every once in a while in the life of a writer, there comes a book that almost seems to write itself. *Which End Is Up?* is one of those books. From the moment I began writing it, I fell in love with Grace and Perry, and couldn't wait to find out what would happen to them. Does that seem strange to you? Did you imagine that the writer *always* knows what is going to happen to her characters?

The truth is, even though I plan each story carefully and have a long and detailed outline, sometimes the characters don't agree with me. That's what happened with Grace and Perry, so I got to experience their story in much the same way you will. I hope you will enjoy it as much as I did.

It was hard to let the Campisi sisters go, and for days after sending the manuscript off to my editor in New York, I walked around in a daze, still thinking about Grace and Perry and wondering how they were doing. I did manage to keep from talking to them, though—at least out loud. This is a habit that drives my husband crazy.

Well, now I've confessed. Writers are a strange breed. We live in our imaginations, and sometimes those imaginary characters and places seem more real to us than the actual world around us. But that's okay. I wouldn't have it any other way.

If you'd like to write me, you can do so via my Web site at www.patriciakay.com. I'd love to hear from you.

Patricia Kay

Acknowledgments

A huge thank-you to all the people who helped bring this book to fruition: Gena Ramsel, who answered questions about Manhattan and Dobbs Ferry; Alaina Richardson, who read every word and kept me honest when it came to lawyers and the law; Christine Wenger and Colleen Thompson, who also read every word and offered invaluable suggestions and comments; my husband, who took over the cooking and just about everything else the last month before the book was due; my special loop of writing buddies (Lois Faye Dyer, Allison Leigh, Cheryl Reavis, Laurie Campbell, Myrna Temte, Christine Flynn, Julia Mozingo and Lisette Belisle) who encouraged and supported me throughout the writing process; and as always, my terrific group of early-morning Curves friends (Linda W., Donna, Adele, Carol, Marsha, Jan, JoAnne, Anna, Linda L. and Connie) who gave me pep talks throughout the writing of this book. I also wish to thank my longtime editor at Silhouette, Gail Chasan, who has been so supportive over the years; Tara Gavin, who bought this book; and my agent, Helen Breitwieser, who continues to believe in me, no matter what.

And a very special thank-you to my readers. It's humbling to realize how much my books mean to you and how they have affected your lives. I love to hear from you and hope you'll keep reading and writing to let me know how you feel about my books.

Dedication

This book is dedicated to sisters everywhere, but especially to my beloved sisters—Gerri Paulicivic, Marge Ford and Norma Johnson. I can't imagine life without you.

PART ONE

New York City

Help one another is part of the religion of sisterhood.
                                        —*Louisa May Alcott*

CHAPTER 1

Fighting the wind and freezing rain, Grace Campisi rounded
the corner of West Sixteenth Street and dug in her purse for
the card key that would open the outer door to her apartment
building. Damn, she hated this weather. When she'd left her
office on this miserable January night, there hadn't been a
vacant cab to be found, so she'd come home on the subway
and had walked the three blocks to her building.

But even though she was exhausted from her twelve-
hour day, most of which had been spent in court, as well
as cold and wet, she smiled when she finally reached the
shelter of the recessed doorway of her new apartment near
Union Square.

She inserted the key, and the release on the lock clicked.
Franklin, the building's security guard, was watching her.
"Evenin', Grace," he said as she pushed open the door.

"Good evening, Franklin." Curious about the odd expression on his swarthy face, she almost said, *Is something*

wrong? but then she saw the figure huddled on a chair in the corner of the small lobby.

Grace's mouth fell open. "Perry?"

"Hi, Grace." Her younger sister grinned sheepishly. "Surprised, huh?"

"That's an understatement." But she shouldn't be. Because showing up unannounced was typical Perry behavior and had been ever since Grace could remember.

Perry struggled to her feet, using the armrest to hoist herself up, and Grace got her second shock of the day. Perry was pregnant! Hugely pregnant—a fact that hadn't been apparent when she was sitting because of the duffel bag she'd held on her lap.

Oh, no, Grace thought.

Perry self-consciously laid her hand on her stomach. "I know. Another surprise."

Her brown eyes, dark and liquid, reminded Grace so much of their father. And even though it had been two years since Sal Campisi Sr. had died of a massive stroke, Grace felt a fresh stab of grief. She had adored her father, and she knew he'd felt the same way about her. If Perry had garnered the lion's share of their mother's attention and love, Grace had been the recipient of their father's.

Fully aware of Franklin's avid curiosity, Grace forced a smile to her face and said, "Let's go up where we can sit and be comfortable, and you can tell me everything."

Turning her smile to the security guard, she said, "Thanks for letting her in, Franklin."

Grabbing the duffel bag, Grace inclined her head toward the elevators behind the guard's station. "This way, Perry."

The sisters didn't talk as the elevator made its slow ascent to the fourth floor of the six-story, thirty-apartment building. Grace's mind was too busy wondering what this visit might mean, and she had no idea what Perry was thinking. She kept stealing glances at her sister, but Perry's face gave away nothing.

On the fourth floor, the elevator came to a jerky stop. Grace grimaced. The antiquated system was the biggest complaint Grace had about the building. Beckoning Perry to follow, Grace led the way to her corner apartment.

Inside, Grace dropped Perry's duffel bag in the living room. "I'm going to change my clothes, okay?"

"Okay," Perry said. She looked around. "This is nice. When did you move here?"

"In September." Which Perry would have known if she'd been in contact, Grace thought with a touch of anger. But the anger quickly dissipated. Perry was Perry. And Grace loved her, warts and all. Besides, Grace wasn't perfect, either, as her mother had reminded her more than once.

"Be right back," Grace said. "Then I'll get us a glass of wine and, if you're hungry, something to eat."

"I'm not supposed to drink."

"Oh. Of course not." Grace should have known that, but hell, *she'd* never been pregnant. And, at forty-two, there wasn't much chance she ever would be. Not that she cared. The only time she'd ever thought about having children had been when Brett... But she didn't want to go there. Brett was gone. That part of her life had been over a long time ago. "Well, a soft drink, then."

Perry nodded and sank onto the sofa. She looked exhausted, her beautiful face pale and showing signs of strain, her eyes clouded with fatigue, her dark, curly hair—God, how Grace had used to envy Perry that hair since her own black hair was stick straight—obviously in need of a good washing and, of course, that cumbersome body, so different from her normally lithe frame.

Grace hurriedly doffed her work clothes and pulled on soft, worn jeans, an old sweatshirt and thick socks. Padding from her bedroom to the kitchen, she set about pouring herself a glass of her favorite Australian Shiraz, then called in to Perry. "Coke okay, Perry?" Maybe pregnant women shouldn't drink Cokes, either.

"Sure," Perry called back.

"You hungry? Want some crackers and cheese?"

"That's okay. I stopped at Angelo's before I came here and had some pizza." Angelo's was their favorite place to go in Little Italy.

So at least Perry wasn't flat broke if she could afford pizza, Grace thought.

A few minutes later, carrying a laden tray into the living room, Grace set it on the distressed-pine coffee table in front of Perry. Then, with a sigh of relief, she sank onto the other end of the sofa and lifted her glass of wine in a toast. "To surprises," she said with a wry smile, "big and small."

Perry smiled back, but Grace could see the wariness in her eyes.

"Okay, spill," Grace said after taking a fortifying swallow of the smooth wine. She reached for a wheat cracker and a slab of cheddar. She hadn't had time for lunch, making do with a Snickers bar and Diet Coke from one of the courthouse vending machines. "What's the story on the pregnancy? And why haven't you said a word about it?"

Perry shrugged. "I was going to."

"But?"

"But I knew you'd be mad and—"

"Christ, Perry, I'm not *mad,* I'm just frustrated that your family is the last to know where you are or what's going on in your life. I mean, hell, we *love* you. For all we know, when we don't hear from you for months and we try to call your last phone number and find it disconnected, you could be *dead.* Why don't you get a damned cell phone, anyway? I'll pay for one if you can't afford it."

Perry swallowed, her eyes tearing up. "You *are* mad."

"Maybe I am," Grace said more calmly. Of course, she was mad. In fact, she'd like to shake Perry sometimes. What did the silly girl *think?* Did she not realize that Grace and her mother worried about her? Maybe their two brothers worried about her, too, although you couldn't prove it by Grace.

What was it Sal had said the last time Grace had talked

to him? *Quit obsessing about her, Grace. She's made her choices and she's living the way she wants to live. Besides, she's twenty-six, a big girl now. Time to stop mothering her.*

Well, obviously *somebody* needed to mother her in terms of trying to steer her in the right direction, Grace thought wearily. Their own mother never said a negative word to Perry or tried to put her on a different path. Although, to be fair, Perry rarely told their mother the truth about anything.

Grace looked at her beautiful sister, at all the unfulfilled promise. "So who's the father?"

Perry shrugged. "It doesn't matter who he is. He's long gone." She avoided Grace's eyes.

As always, Grace was torn between love and exasperation. Why did Perry continue to do things like this? Every single man she'd ever hooked up with—and there had been many—had been a total loser. They'd either used her as a punching bag, freeloaded off her when she'd had a job or left her. This was the second time Perry had gotten pregnant by a man who'd taken off. The last time, she had miscarried in her fourth month, but obviously, this time she seemed to be okay.

"When are you due?" Grace asked.

Another shrug. "In a week or so, I think."

"You *think*? Perry, have you seen a doctor?"

"I've gone a couple of times."

Oh, God. "Have you been taking prenatal vitamins? Watching what you eat? Taking care of yourself?"

The miserable look on Perry's face was enough to tell

Grace everything she needed to know. She stifled a sigh. "I don't suppose you have any health insurance."

Perry shook her head. Her gaze finally met Grace's, and Grace could see the fear in her eyes.

"What are you planning to do?" Grace said more gently.

Perry swallowed. "I—I was hoping I could stay with you until I have the baby and...can get on my feet again."

"How'd you even know how to find me?" Grace asked, stalling for time.

"I called Mom."

"Does she know about the pregnancy?"

Perry shook her head again. When a few long moments of silence went by, she drained her glass of Coke, then said, "I know it's a lot to ask, Grace, but I—I'm broke, and I don't have anywhere else to go."

Grace wanted to say no. She loved Perry, but how could she have her here, probably for months? And not just her. A baby, too. *Where will I put them?* she thought wildly, her mind spinning. Her apartment *did* have two bedrooms, but the second one was very small and Grace had her exercise equipment in it.

And then there was Doug. Doug Frasier, her lover. He spent a lot of time at her place. They would have no privacy at all if Perry was there.

I can't. I just can't have her here.

And yet, how could she turn her sister away? Their brothers certainly wouldn't take her in, even if Perry would consider going to them, and Grace knew she wouldn't.

And their mother couldn't. She lived in a retirement community in Florida, in an apartment she shared with her sister. Even if they'd had the room, the community didn't allow children except for limited visits. Grace would have to do it. "All right," she finally said, "you can stay here."

Perry leaned forward and threw her arms around Grace. "Oh, thank you, Grace. Thank you. I—I promise it won't be for long."

Grace closed her eyes. She could feel the tremors in Perry's body. She was scared. Love constricted Grace's throat. "Don't worry, honey. Everything will be okay." But even as she said the words, she knew they weren't true.

In fact, Perry's life was a mess, and from past experience, Grace was afraid it would stay a mess.

She hoped she was wrong.

She hoped that somehow, this time, Perry would be able to cope. That she'd have her baby, find a job and child care and get her act together.

Because if she didn't…

But Grace couldn't go there. Right now, all she had the strength to do was hold her sister and keep telling her everything would work out just fine.

Perry couldn't get comfortable. It wasn't the fault of the daybed, which looked new and had a good mattress. It was her pregnancy and the fact that her back ached constantly and her feet were swollen and her stomach was so enormous.

Why? she asked herself for the millionth time. *Why did*

I do something so stupid? Why did I stop taking my birth-control pills? Just because Don and I had split up and I was upset didn't mean I was never going to have sex again. Now what am I going to do? How am I going to take care of a baby?

The tears that had been so close to the surface these past months threatened again. Perry let them come. She knew she was weak, that if Grace heard her crying, she'd probably just roll her eyes in disgust, but Perry couldn't seem to help it. Thinking about a baby and everything it entailed terrified her.

If only Don…

But Perry knew there was no point in thinking about Don. Even though they'd gotten back together, he'd made his feelings really clear when she'd realized she was pregnant. He didn't want some other man's baby. "It's me or the kid," he'd said. "Take your choice."

He'd wanted her to have an abortion. For about two minutes, Perry had actually considered it. But even though she hadn't been in love with the baby's father— a sailor named Johnny—she knew she couldn't just get rid of the baby.

Her baby.

That was the key.

This was her baby.

Maybe it was her Catholic upbringing. That whole guilt thing. Perry didn't know. All she knew was, from the time she was a child, she couldn't kill anything. Not a spider. Not a beetle. Not even a wasp. Nothing.

Don had shrugged when she'd told him. "If you change your mind, babe, you know where to find me."

Yes, but he wouldn't wait forever. Don wasn't the kind of guy to be without a woman for long. Just like Perry wasn't the kind of woman who could get along without a man.

Why can't I be more like Grace?

Grace didn't need anybody. She never had. From Perry's earliest memories, Grace had been self-sufficient. Even when she'd fall down and scrape her knees or get stung by a bee, she never ran into the house crying for their mother. Come to think of it, she hardly ever cried, period. She'd just take care of whatever happened by herself.

If it were Grace having a baby, she'd put it up for adoption. Of course, the thought itself was ridiculous. There was no way Grace would *ever* have gotten pregnant unless she'd wanted to. Perry cringed just thinking what Grace would say if she knew about the night Perry had gotten pregnant. It was a miracle Perry had even survived that night, she'd been so wasted.

That was the biggest difference between Perry and Grace. Perry did crazy stuff; she leaped without looking. Grace looked first, thought about the consequences, then did the sensible thing. She was always in control.

Perry dried her tears. Maybe she *would* put the baby up for adoption. She knew that's what Grace thought she should do. It made sense.

And yet…how could she stand knowing her baby was out there somewhere, but never get to see her or him?

Perry knew it was probably stupid and selfish of her to feel that way. If only she could change Don's mind....

Oh, shit, she had to quit thinking about Don. He wasn't an option.

She only had two choices. Keep the baby and try to raise it herself. Or give it up for adoption.

And no amount of thinking or crying or wishing for impossible things was going to change that.

One's sister is a part of one's essential self, an eternal presence of one's heart and soul and memory.

—*Susan Cabill*

CHAPTER 2

"You did *what?*"

Although Grace had known Doug wouldn't be thrilled to find out Perry would be spending the next couple of months with her, his tone immediately put her back up. "I said," she replied stiffly, "that I told Perry she could stay with me until she gets on her feet."

"And what if she never does?"

"That's my problem, isn't it?"

He stared at her. Around them, the lunch crowd at Macy's Cellar Bar and Grill talked noisily, but Grace and Doug might have been on an island for all the attention they paid them. After a moment, he shrugged. Turning his attention to his club sandwich, he ate silently.

Grace's anger evaporated. After all, hadn't Doug only voiced her own concerns? And the situation with Perry *wasn't* just Grace's problem, because Perry's presence would impact her relationship with Doug. In fact, for the fore-seeable future, if the two of them wanted privacy, Grace would have to go to his apartment.

And she hated doing that.

Not only was it inconvenient, but she wasn't comfort-able there. The apartment was too impersonal and cold with its stark white walls, black, chrome and glass furnish-ings and violently abstract paintings. Grace might have been known as a shark at work, but at home she liked comfort and warmth.

Sighing, she said, "I'm sorry, Doug. You're right. But what else could I have done? I mean, she literally just showed up on my doorstep. With no job and no money."

Putting his sandwich down, he wiped his mouth with his napkin, then met her gaze. "You could have rented her an apartment. Hell, Grace, I'd've been happy to chip in for half."

"I thought of that, but I just couldn't do it."

"Why not?"

"I don't know. It seemed…mean. As if I don't care about her. And I do."

"There comes a time when you have to think about yourself."

"I know, but she's my *sister*, Doug."

"I'm aware of that. But haven't you told me yourself that she's a screwup? She can't keep a job, she has lousy judgment in men, she's always in some kind of trouble."

"Yes, but—"

"The longer you keep bailing her out, Grace, the longer she'll keep screwing up."

Grace knew no matter how she tried to explain, he'd never understand. He was an only child. A much-indulged only child, born to older parents who had given up ever having a child of their own. They'd pretty much given him anything he wanted. He even admitted it, saying he knew he was a self-centered person, and he made no apologies for it. "That's why we get along so well," he'd said, smiling at her. "We know what we want out of life, and we go for it."

When he'd said that, Grace hadn't disagreed, because essentially, he was right. Yet he wasn't one hundred percent right, because Grace *did* care about her family, sometimes much to her consternation. And she especially cared about Perry. Maybe no man could ever understand that special bond between sisters.

That was the bottom line.

Perry was her sister, with everything that relationship meant. And no matter what she'd done, Grace simply couldn't turn her back on her.

"Are you going to finish your salad?" Doug asked.

Grace blinked. She'd been so lost in her thoughts, she'd almost forgotten he was there. "No, I'm done." She pushed her plate away.

He motioned to their waiter, then asked for the bill.

When they parted, he kissed her cheek but said nothing about seeing her again, even though he'd just returned from a week-long conference. Under normal circumstances, he would have been eager to get her into bed.

Fighting depression, Grace hurried back to her office. She had a full afternoon ahead of her and she was determined not to think about her personal problems—that was not the way to secure the partnership she coveted—but that vow turned out to be easier made than accomplished. Because no matter how hard she tried, throughout the remainder of the day she had a hard time concentrating, and by six o'clock—early for her—she packed up her briefcase and headed for home.

She heard the TV laugh track before she'd even inserted her key into the lock of her apartment door. She told herself to chill—so what if Perry watched TV all day long? What else was she supposed to do this close to her due date? Still, Grace gritted her teeth at the sight of Perry's feet propped on top of the coffee table. Grace glanced around, cringing inwardly at the potato-chip crumbs littering the sofa, at the sweating glass half filled with Coke that sat on the end table without virtue of a coaster, at the TV remote that had fallen from Perry's fingers and lay on the floor. Perry herself was asleep, her mouth slightly open, her chest rising and falling as she snored softly.

Shaking her head, Grace walked over to the sofa and picked up the remote. She pressed the off button and blessed silence filled the apartment. Perry, oblivious, slept on. Grace reached for the Coke-filled glass and, walking into the kitchen, placed it in the sink. Then she headed for her bedroom where she changed into warm-ups.

After debating whether to climb onto her stationary bike or pour herself a glass of wine and crash, she decided she needed the wine more than she needed the exercise. Besides, it was time to talk to Perry. She'd been at the apartment for a week now, and they had yet to discuss the future.

When Grace returned to the living room, Perry stirred, yawned hugely, then said, "Hey, Grace." She rubbed her eyes. "I didn't hear you come in."

Grace curled into the big armchair that was her favorite place to sit in the evenings. "You were dead to the world."

"I know. I'm always so tired lately."

Grace nodded and drank some of her wine. "Perr, can we talk?"

"Sure." Although Perry answered readily enough, her eyes had turned wary.

"I was just wondering if you've given any thought to what you're going to do after the baby comes."

Perry picked at a loose thread on the throw covering her legs. "I guess I'll need to get a job."

"Doing what?" As far as Grace knew, the only jobs Perry had held in the past eight years since graduating from high school had been as a waitress or a bartender.

"I don't know," Perry said uncertainly. "Bartending pays best, but—"

"What?"

"Well, most of those jobs are at night."

Grace nodded. "I imagine it would be hard to find child care at night."

"Yeah, that's kinda what I thought."

"Do you plan to stay here in New York?"

"I—I don't know."

"Perry, you have to start making some kind of plan. You're going to have a *baby*."

"Don't you think I *know* that?" Perry cried. "I just, I don't know what to *do*."

Grace sighed deeply. After another swallow of her wine, she said softly, "What about adoption? Have you considered that?"

Perry nodded slowly.

"And?"

"I don't know if I can do it, Grace. Just…just give the baby away to strangers."

"Even if they can give the baby a better life?"

Perry didn't answer for a long minute. When she did, her voice was impassioned. "But how will I *know* if my baby is having a better life? If I could give her…or him…to someone I know…if I could just be *sure*… I mean you hear all the time about people who are mean to kids…" Her voice trailed off miserably.

Grace tried to put herself into Perry's shoes, but it was almost impossible. Grace had never wanted children. Well, maybe that wasn't entirely true. When she'd been engaged to Brett…but that had been so many years ago it was almost another lifetime.

Brett Halliday.

She could still see him. Tall, lean, blond, blue-eyed, gorgeous. The antithesis of her Italian brothers and cousins. Oh, how she'd loved him.

They'd met in college, when Grace had been a sophomore and he'd been a senior. She'd been in the library, studying, and had dropped her pencil. He'd been walking by and had picked it up. When he'd handed it to her, their eyes had met. And that was it. The oldest cliché in the book. He'd told her later he'd known immediately she was the girl he wanted to spend the rest of his life with and she'd admitted she felt the same way.

By the time Brett had graduated, they were engaged and planning to be married. Then just six months later, Brett was gone, killed in an automobile accident while driving back to graduate school after spending a weekend with her.

Grace had been devastated. She'd walked around like a zombie for weeks. It had taken her the better part of two years to get over losing him. And once she finally had, she'd made the conscious decision never to risk her heart again. From that day on, all of her passion and energy and commitment had been lavished on her career, which was something concrete she could control.

Telling herself she had no regrets, she wrenched her thoughts back to Perry. "What about the father? You said he was long gone. Does he know about the baby?"

Perry shook her head.

"Why not?"

"Because I didn't know I was pregnant when he left. He's a sailor, Grace. He's gone to sea. Besides, I don't love him. I never did. He was just someone to have fun with for a couple of days. The cousin of some girl I used to work with."

Grace wanted to say, *Why weren't you using some kind of birth control?* but she didn't. What was the use? Perry was pregnant, and nothing was going to change that fact now. "So there's no help from that quarter."

"No."

"Well, what about when he comes back? This is his baby, too. Maybe he'd *want* to be involved."

Perry shook her head stubbornly. "He probably wouldn't even believe me. Besides, I don't even know his last name."

"But if you know his cousin…"

"I have no idea where she is now."

"What's her name?"

"Glenda."

"What's her last name?"

"I'm not sure. I think it's Lewis. But she was getting married, so that wouldn't be her name now, anyway."

"We can track her down. I'll hire a private detective."

Perry shook her head. "No, Grace, I don't want to do that. I just want to forget about her cousin. He was just a sailor I partied with. Him and a whole bunch of other people. I mean, we were all wasted that night."

Grace sighed and got up to refill her wineglass. Wasn't this just typical of Perry? Grace had a feeling Perry wasn't even sure this particular sailor *was* her baby's father. She thought about how Perry had said, *we were all wasted that night.* Had she had sex with more than one sailor on the night her baby had been conceived? Grace hated thinking such negative things about her sister, but good grief, Perry asked for it with her bad judgment and irresponsible actions.

Grace finally returned to the living room. For a long moment she studied Perry's downcast head. "If you could, would you like to stay in New York?" she asked gently.

"I don't know," Perry said, looking up. "Maybe."

"Okay, let's say you do stay, and after the baby's born, you found yourself a good bartending job. Child care is really expensive here, and the cost of nice apartments are out of sight. I just don't see how you could possibly make enough money to support yourself *and* a baby."

"I know." Her face was bleak.

"Maybe adoption really *is* your best bet."

"Maybe." But she didn't sound at all sure. Suddenly she looked up. "You haven't changed your mind, have you, Grace? You'll still let me stay here until I figure it all out?"

"No, I haven't changed my mind. But this has to be temporary, Perry. This apartment's barely big enough for you and me, let alone a baby."

"I know."

That helpless sound was back in Perry's voice. It was a sound that made Grace want to scream on the one hand and hug Perry on the other hand. Hardening her heart, she said, "Another thing…when are you planning to tell Mom?"

"I..." Perry swallowed. "I'll call her."

"When? After the baby's born?"

"No, I'll call her before. I still have a week, you know."

"Well, from what I read, even though first babies are often late, they have been known to show up early also." For the past week, Grace had been doing some research online.

"I'll call her tomorrow."

"Promise?"

Perry didn't answer for a moment. Finally she said, "Yeah, I promise."

Their mother, Stella Zlotnick Campisi, lived in Seacrest, Florida, in an apartment she shared with her older sister, Mutt. She adored Perry.

"I don't understand why you've been so reluctant to tell her, especially if you plan to keep the baby. She's always forgiven you anything." This last was said wryly.

It was too bad their mother no longer had a home of her own, Grace thought. Perry could have gone to live with Stella, and even though Stella couldn't have cared for the baby on her own, Perry could have afforded child care if she wasn't paying rent.

Dream on, Grace....

Grace sighed again. She seemed to be doing a lot of that lately. "Well, I guess we'll figure out something," she said, draining her wineglass. "You hungry?"

"Starving," Perry said, her face brightening.

"Feel like Chinese?"

"Sure."

"Cashew Chicken and Beef and Broccoli okay?"

"Yeah, and get some of those fried dumplings, too, okay?"

Grace headed for the kitchen to pour another glass of wine and to call Chan's, her favorite for takeout. Maybe tomorrow she should ask Jamie, her secretary, to start checking into possible child-care options, because she doubted Perry would do anything until she absolutely had to, and it might take awhile to find a place that was good *and* that she could afford. Although, Grace fully intended to help Perry out financially, if that was what it took for her to live in a place of her own.

After phoning in their food order, Grace carried her wine back to the living room.

"Don called today," Perry said after Grace sat down.

Grace frowned. "Don?"

"My boyfriend."

"I'm confused. What boyfriend?"

"I thought I told you about him."

"No, Perry," Grace said as patiently as she could, even though she was back to wanting to strangle her sister, "you didn't."

"We…we've been together about a year."

"But…"

"I know what you're thinking. You're thinking if we've been together, then why was I messing around with a sailor."

"Why *were* you?"

"Because Don and I had had a fight, and he'd walked out

on me. I—I was upset and I thought it was over. So when Glenda invited me to come to that party with her, I went."

"And the rest is history," Grace muttered.

"Anyway, we went back together a few weeks later."

"So why aren't you with him now, then?"

"He…he doesn't want to raise somebody else's baby."

"I see."

"Don't say it that way, Grace. He can't help how he feels."

Grace started to make a sarcastic comment about him sounding like a real prince of a guy, but at the last second she stopped herself, remembering Doug. He wouldn't want to raise someone else's child, either. "So why did Don call you?" she finally asked.

"He's thinking about moving to Vegas. He said they're having a building boom there and since he works construction, he should be able to get as much work as he wants."

"I'd think he'd be able to get lots of work in the San Diego area, too."

"He's not in San Diego right now. He's in L.A."

"Then how'd you meet him?"

"He was living in San Diego when I met him. Cookie introduced me to him."

Grace was totally lost now. "Who's Cookie?"

"I told you about her."

"No, you didn't. When would you tell me? I haven't talked to you since last March."

"She's my best friend. *Was* my best friend. We worked together for over a year."

"What happened that she's no longer your best friend?"

"Oh, you know. We had a falling out."

Grace stifled a sigh. None of Perry's relationships survived very long. "So your boyfriend is moving to Vegas?"

"Yeah, I guess."

"Well, if you decide to go back to California instead of staying here in New York, that might be a good thing. It might make it easier for you if he's not around."

Perry nodded, but her face was bleak. "I wish..." Perry's eyes, when they met Grace's, were swimming with tears.

Now Grace felt bad. "I know."

"No, you don't." Perry pulled a wadded up Kleenex out of her pocket and wiped her eyes. "You're smart and strong and clever. You've always done everything right. And I've never done anything right. So how *could* you know?"

"Perry..."

"What's wrong with me, Grace?" she cried. "Why do I always mess up?"

For the life of her, Grace couldn't think of anything comforting to say. If she said Perry was wrong, Perry would know it was a lie.

Finally she said, "Look, it's never too late to change your life. There are women who go to college in their sixties, women who scrub toilets to support entire families, women who do whatever it takes to improve their lives. You can do that, too."

"You could do it. I'm not sure about me."

"I'll help you. If you'll promise to try, I promise I'll help you."

"I—" She bowed her head. "I—I'll do the best I can, Grace."

And then the doorbell rang, and their food arrived, and the subject of Perry's life was dropped. But their conversation hovered at the back of Grace's mind, even after Perry had gone to bed and Grace sat reading a deposition taken by one of the other associates.

What would she do if Perry couldn't get her act together? How long was she prepared to have her sister here, especially once the baby arrived?

Grace didn't know.

What she did know was that in the coming weeks, she would need all the understanding and patience she possessed.

Sisters function as safety nets in a chaotic world simply by being there for each other.

—*Carol Saline*

CHAPTER 3

Grace was dreaming. The managing partner at her firm, Wallace Finn, had called all the associates into the big conference room and Grace knew the new partnership was going to be announced. She also knew she had won the position, because Wallace had already told her. When she arrived in the conference room, bottles of champagne were already chilling, and there were several platters of hors d'oeuvres on the table.

Wallace smiled at her as she entered the room, beckoning her to his side. She could see from the faces of the other associates that they realized why they'd been called in. She carefully avoided the stony gaze of Jack Townsend, who had been her primary rival for the past year. As her triumph washed over her in warm waves, she kept her own expression pleasant. No need to wear her victory like a trophy. Everyone there knew what a coup she'd pulled off.

To be made a full partner at Finn, Braddock and Morgan at the age of forty-two was no small accomplishment.

Wallace had just finished making his announcement—to a nice round of applause—and had turned to her to offer a toast when she heard the scream. Frowning, wondering who on earth had screamed, she looked around the room.

"Grace! Grace!"

Grace bolted up. "Ohmigod! Perry." Dream forgotten, she jumped out of bed, grabbed her robe and dashed into the spare room where Perry was sleeping on the daybed. "What's wrong?" she cried, heart pounding in fear.

"My water broke," Perry said.

And then Grace saw how wet she was, how wet the bedclothes were.

"I—I didn't realize I was in labor," Perry said, her eyes frightened. "M-my back was hurting, and I was just getting up to go get some Advil or something when it happened."

Grace had researched childbirth thoroughly, including a careful reading of the instructions given to Perry by the obstetrician Grace had found for her. "Have you started having contractions yet?"

"I—I don't think so."

Grace nodded. From everything she'd read, contractions would begin within ten to twelve hours for a first-time birth. "I don't think there's anything we need to do then, except get you into some dry clothes."

"Are you sure?"

Grace knew Perry was scared. "I'm pretty sure, but if you

want to go to the hospital, we can go. I just think they'll probably tell you to go home if you're not having any contractions yet."

Perry worried her lower lip. Then she sighed. "Okay, we'll wait."

Perry's contractions started at six o'clock, just about the time Grace normally awakened. Although Grace had work piled up to her ears at the office, she knew there was no way she could leave Perry on her own today. So after showering, she dressed in jeans, a warm sweater, socks and comfortable walking shoes. Then she fixed herself some breakfast. By eight o'clock, Perry's contractions were eleven minutes apart, and Grace decided it was time to leave for the hospital.

It was after nine by the time Grace had finished signing all the forms saying she'd be responsible for Perry's bills. When an attendant put Perry into a wheelchair to take her up to delivery, Grace told Perry she'd join her there in a few minutes. "First I have to call my office."

"You are going to stay with me, aren't you?" Perry's voice wobbled. She was obviously terrified.

Grace suppressed a sigh. "Perry, I *said* I would stay."

"I'm sorry, Grace. It's just that I'm—"

"I know. You're scared."

Perry swallowed and blinked back tears. "Yeah."

Grace gave the attendant a smile. "Go ahead and take her. I'll be there soon."

Once they were on their way, Grace walked to the end

of the hallway where it was quieter, took out her cell phone and pressed 1 on her speed dial.

Her secretary picked up on the second ring. After explaining the situation, Grace said, "Ask Ken to sit in on the Cox Insurance Company meeting this morning."

"Okay," Jamie said. "But what about tomorrow? You're due in court at ten."

"I'll be there."

"What about your appointment with Andrew Cutter?"

"Shit. I forgot about it. Um, call him and ask if we can reschedule for tomorrow or Friday."

"And if he can't make it then? His tour's starting soon, you know."

"Just ask him, Jamie. If he says he can't, tell him I'll give him a call later today, and we'll work something out. If I have to, I'll meet with him tonight."

"You don't want me to see if Jack can talk to him today instead?"

"Absolutely not." That was the last thing Grace wanted. Jack Townsend would love to get his teeth into the Andrew Cutter case, which involved copyright infringement and had the potential for a multimillion-dollar payoff, forty percent of which would belong to the firm. And if the case ended up going to trial, the firm could earn as much as fifty percent, not to mention the hundreds of billable hours for the associates and legal assistants.

"Okay."

After hanging up, Grace wondered why Jamie would even ask her such a question. Her secretary was certainly smart enough to realize Jack Townsend was just waiting for the opportunity to upstage Grace. Could Jack have approached Jamie? Grace knew she was being paranoid, but when a partnership was up for grabs, people would do just about anything to secure it, especially someone like Jack, who was a bit oily. And Jamie could be naive. *Damn*. Perry *would* have to go into labor today. Well, maybe by two o'clock everything would be over, and Grace could make the meeting with Andrew Cutter after all.

On that thought, she headed for the elevators.

"Mom?"

"Grace?"

"You weren't in bed, were you?"

"No, Aunt Mutt and I were just sitting here watching *The Tonight Show* and having a nice glass of port. Why? Is there something wrong?"

"Don't worry. Nothing bad has happened." Grace hesitated. There was no way to prepare her mother, so she might as well just tell her. "But this will come as kind of a shock, I'm afraid. Less than an hour ago Perry gave birth to an eight-pound, three-ounce baby girl."

For a moment, there was silence. Then her mother said in a stunned voice, "Sh-she had a baby?"

"Yes. A healthy, beautiful baby." The baby *was* beautiful. Grace had seen her only minutes after she'd been born, and contrary to what she'd expected, the baby wasn't scrawny or red or wrinkled. She had fat little cheeks, huge eyes and silky black hair. Grace was surprised at how the sight of the baby had affected her, for she'd never considered herself a "baby" person, but she'd actually become teary-eyed when she'd seen her niece.

"B-but why didn't she tell me she was pregnant?"

"She was going to call you today, but the baby came early, before she had a chance."

"How…? Has she been *staying* with you?"

"Yes. She showed up at my apartment a week ago."

"That's why she called for your address," Stella said thoughtfully.

"Yes."

"Who's the father? Is *he* there, too?"

Grace sighed. "The baby's father is…not in the picture, Mom."

Now she heard her mother sigh. "Oh, my poor Perry. What is she going to do?"

"I don't know. She's considering placing the baby for adoption." Might as well prepare her mother. When Stella didn't say anything, Grace said, "Mom? You okay?"

"No, Grace, I'm not okay. I'm upset. She should have *told* me."

"I think she was scared to."

"Scared to? Scared of *me?*"

"She wants you to think well of her."

"As if I wouldn't!" Grace's mother said indignantly.

That's true. It's only me you don't think well of. "Well, you know now," Grace said.

"Do you think I should try to come?"

Grace knew how uncomfortable it was for her mother to travel, especially in the winter when her arthritic hip was always worse. "It's not necessary. Perry is fine. In fact, she'll probably be sent home in a day or so. She'll call you then, okay?"

"O-okay. Tell her I love her, Grace. And tell her not to even *think* of giving her baby away. The very idea!"

Grace closed her eyes. That was so easy for her mother to say. Was *she* going to raise the baby? "Even if that's the best thing for the baby?"

"But it's *not* the best thing, Grace. How can you say that?"

And how can you not?

"Perry's not like you, Grace," her mother said. "She'd regret giving away her baby. It would haunt her for the rest of her life."

After they hung up, Grace thought about how nothing ever changed. Her mother would always find a way to hit the bull's-eye when she threw her poison darts.

"All hell broke loose here yesterday afternoon," Jamie said, laying a stack of files in Grace's in-box.

Grace had a headache this morning, which even two Advil hadn't seemed to help. "Why? What happened?"

"Dixie Burton showed up and made a scene."

Grace rolled her eyes. Dixie and Peter Burton, one of the associates, were in the middle of a nasty divorce.

"Mr. Finn wasn't pleased," Jamie continued.

"I'll bet." Wallace Finn was ultraconservative and had made his views on divorce well known.

After first glancing behind her to make sure the door was closed, Jamie added, "I overheard him telling Peter that if he couldn't keep his personal problems at home, he should think about staying home permanently."

"Oops," Grace said.

Peter Burton was a nice guy. Grace felt sorry for him. But Wallace Finn was right. Personal problems had no place at the office. Especially *this* office. As soon as the thought formed, she felt a little flicker of unease. She'd allowed her personal problems to infringe on the office yesterday when she'd had to cancel that appointment with Andrew Cutter. She frowned. Cutter hadn't been happy, although he'd agreed to make time for her tomorrow morning. He'd refused to come to the office, though, saying she'd need to come out to Long Island. She guessed she didn't blame him.

After Jamie went back out to her desk, Grace plunged herself into reviewing her notes in preparation for court this morning. She had just finished and was packing her briefcase when Jamie buzzed her, saying Perry was on the line.

"Hi, Perry," Grace said, anchoring the phone on her shoulder while she continued stuffing papers into the briefcase.

"Hi, Grace."

"How're you feeling this morning?"

"I'm okay."

Grace frowned. "You don't sound okay."

"I'm just tired and sore."

"Well, rest, then."

"Yeah. I'll try. Uh, what time are you coming today?"

"To the hospital?"

"Yeah."

"I wasn't planning to come until tonight. I've got a job, you know. In fact, if I don't get going soon, I'm going to be late for court."

"Oh. I'm sorry. I-I'll let you go."

"It's okay. But listen, Perry, don't forget to give Mom a call this morning. She's really anxious to talk to you."

"Will they let me make a long-distance call from my hospital room?"

"Yes. They'll just put it on the bill."

"Oh. Okay. Well, I guess I'll see you around seven, then? And Grace? Could you bring me some magazines or something?"

"Sure." Knowing her sister, Grace figured she'd want fluff like *People* or *Us*.

Despite what she'd told Perry, it was more like eight-thirty before Grace made it to the hospital. Perry had been put in a semiprivate room, and when Grace arrived, she was sitting up in bed holding the baby.

Grace leaned over and kissed Perry's cheek, then impulsively kissed the baby's forehead. Her skin was incredibly soft and, once again, Grace felt a tug of love that surprised her.

"We can go home tomorrow," Perry said.

"So soon?"

"Yeah, my doctor said she'd sign the release in the morning."

"Since you said *we*, does that mean you've made a decision?"

Perry's dark eyes met Grace's. She nodded. "I—I want to keep her, Grace. I just…I can't give her away. And by the way," she added softly, "her name is Emily. Emily Grace Campisi." She smiled. "I wanted her to have your name."

Grace was touched, even as she wondered if this was really the best thing for the baby. She also wondered just how much Perry's decision had been due to their mother's feelings about the subject. "Thanks. Um, what time tomorrow?"

"I don't know. I guess it depends on when Dr. Majors makes rounds. This morning she was here before eight. All I know is I'll probably have to be out of here by noon."

Damn. What was Grace going to do? She had to be out on Long Island at ten. There was no way she'd be back before noon. "Perry, you might have to wait a couple of hours for me." She explained about the appointment with Andrew Cutter. "Or else take a cab to the apartment by yourself."

At Perry's stricken look, Grace thought quickly, then

said, "Or maybe I could just ask my secretary Jamie to come and get you."

Grace knew she was walking on eggshells here. Using her secretary to take care of personal business for her was a no-no. Now if she were a partner, she might be able to get away with it. But while she was striving to attain that partnership, she needed to keep her nose clean. The fact that Jamie really liked running personal errands because it got her away from the office for a while made no difference, at least not to the Powers That Be.

But what choice did she have? Using Jamie would be the lesser of two evils. "That would be okay, wouldn't it?" she asked Perry.

"I guess."

"And I'll come straight to the apartment after my appointment," Grace promised. "Make sure you're settled in okay before I go back to work."

Perry nodded.

Later, as Grace wearily took off for home, she thought about what she'd committed herself to. Having Perry and the baby with her was going to be even harder than she'd imagined. It was already impacting her job performance. That was going to have to stop. Even though Grace felt guilty thinking this when Perry was so vulnerable right now, Grace had to harden her heart and put herself first. After all, Perry would move on, but Grace would have to live with her success or failure on the job. So after tomorrow, Grace could not let Perry's or the baby's presence in her life interfere with her career again.

The question was how could she make sure that didn't happen?

"You have to put the nipple into her mouth and keep it there until she really latches on."

Perry glared at the lactation specialist. "It hurts."

"I know it hurts at first, but it's important that you learn to nurse your baby. There's no substitute for a mother's milk. Even if you only nurse for a couple of weeks, your baby's immune system will be boosted and she'll be a lot healthier. Now try again."

Perry tried. But Emily couldn't seem to get any milk. So she cried, and then Perry cried. And all the while, that hateful woman stood there with that disapproving look on her face. Perry was sick of people looking at her that way. No matter what she did, somebody thought she could do it better.

I'm so tired. I just want to go to sleep. A tear trickled down her face and she turned her head away from the woman's accusatory gaze.

"Perry," the woman said.

"Go away."

"Now, Perry…"

Suddenly Perry didn't give a damn what anyone thought. She was the one who'd just had a baby. She was the one whose nipples hurt like crazy. She was the one who had cramps and a sore bottom. She was the one who might have to give her baby away. Not this stupid woman with her stupid *you're not trying, Perry* bullshit. "Go away," she said again. She picked up the call button and pressed it.

When the nurse at the nurse's station came in, Perry said, "I need a bottle of formula for my baby."

"Dr. Goodall isn't going to be happy," the woman said stiffly. Dr. Goodall was the staff pediatrician.

"Both of you can go to hell," Perry muttered. Then she turned her back on the woman's affronted expression and didn't move until she heard the woman leave the room.

If you don't understand how a woman could both love her sister dearly and want to wring her neck at the same time, then you were probably an only child.
—*Linda Sunshine*

CHAPTER 4

Perry and the baby hadn't been home two days when Grace knew she was going to have to do something. It was obvious that Perry couldn't manage on her own. She seemed overwhelmed by the responsibility of taking care of Emily. Perry looked panicked when Grace left for work, and when Grace returned at the end of the day, she walked into chaos. The apartment was a mess, Emily cried all the time and Perry cried right along with her.

"I don't know what I'm doing *wrong!*" she wailed to Grace. "Why does she cry so much?"

Grace didn't have any answers. What did *she* know about babies? What she *did* know was that things couldn't continue like this. She was as exhausted as Perry, because the baby kept them both awake half the night.

After a stern talk from the hospital pediatrician, which

had made Perry feel guilty, she had gone back to trying to breast-feed Emily. It was no longer painful for her now that her breast milk had fully come in, so both she and Grace felt her attempts were successful.

But the new pediatrician disagreed. "She's probably not getting enough milk," she said when Grace called her. "I know the conventional wisdom is mothers should breast-feed no matter what, but I think a full baby is a happy baby, so let's try formula."

So Perry began bottle-feeding Emily. That helped the baby sleep for longer periods of time, but it didn't do much to help Perry who, when she wasn't feeding the baby, didn't seem to want to do anything except sleep herself or watch television.

Grace knew Perry was depressed, but she didn't know what to do about it.

In desperation, she called Perry's obstetrician, who directed her to a nonprofit agency that specialized in counseling new mothers. "They probably won't give you free help," the doctor said, "but they'll point you in the right direction."

"That's all I want," Grace said, thanking her.

The woman at the agency told Grace her best bet would be to hire a baby nurse to come in and stay while she was at work. "A good nurse will not only help with the care of the baby, she'll teach your sister how to manage better, which will probably alleviate her depression." She gave Grace the name and number of a service that could provide her with a private-duty nurse. "Since she's no longer nursing, if that doesn't help, ask her obstetrician to prescribe medication for depression."

"I'll do that," Grace said, thanking her.

An hour later, Grace had made arrangements for a baby nurse to start the following day. She'd winced at the cost— her emergency savings account was dangerously low due to Perry's hospital and doctor bills—but they wouldn't need the nurse forever. Telling herself this situation was only temporary, that soon Perry would be feeling better and Emily would adjust and things would settle down, Grace tried to relax with a cup of hot chocolate while Perry and the baby were both sleeping.

She'd no sooner settled herself into her favorite chair when her cell phone rang. The caller ID showed the caller to be Doug. This was the first time he'd called her since their disastrous luncheon eight days earlier.

"Hello," she said coolly.

"Hi, Grace. How're things going?"

"Okay."

"How's your sister doing?"

As if you care. "She's fine. She had the baby on Friday."

"And how're you holding up?"

"I'm tired. It's hard to get a full night's sleep with a newborn in the apartment."

"I'm not surprised."

She smiled wryly. He wouldn't even pretend to be sympathetic. But that was Doug. What you saw was what you got. He had told her once that he didn't waste time pretending concern he didn't feel, that most people's problems were brought on by poor decisions, not by circumstances. When she'd challenged him, saying she didn't think kids who had cancer had brought on their disease by poor decisions, he'd said that was different and that she knew what he'd meant. At the time, she'd decided she was being too hard on him. He was pragmatic. There was nothing wrong with that.

"I'd like to see you," he said. His voice softened. "I've missed you."

"I've missed you, too." But had she, really? Her response had been automatic, but the truth was, there was so much on her plate right now, she hadn't had much time to even think about him, much less miss him.

"How about dinner together Saturday night? Afterward, we can come here to my place. Of course," he added, chuckling, "I can't promise you a *full* night's sleep here, either."

Dinner out and a quiet night that included some great sex was suddenly tempting, but Grace hesitated. Could she chance leaving Perry alone all night?

"What's wrong?" he said when the silence lengthened. "Don't you want to?"

Grace sighed. "I'd love to. I'm just not sure Perry will be okay on her own."

"Christ, Grace, how old is Perry? Twenty-six? Twenty-seven?"

"Twenty-six."

"Old enough to take care of herself all the time, not to mention one night."

"The thing is, she's depressed."

"Maybe if she'd thought before getting pregnant, she wouldn't *be* depressed."

"Yes, but she *did* get pregnant, and now there's a baby to consider."

"So what're you going to do? Hold her hand forever?"

Grace gritted her teeth. This discussion would get them nowhere. "Doug, can we please just agree to disagree where Perry's concerned? I've got a headache, and I really don't want to talk about this."

"Fine by me. What about Saturday? Can you make it or not?"

She almost told him to forget it. She wasn't sure she still wanted to go. But she knew that was being petty. "What time and where do you want to meet?"

"How about Chan's at eight? I'll make a reservation."

Chan's was one of Grace's favorite restaurants. He was trying. "All right. I'll be there."

Grace disconnected the call and sat thinking about the conversation. It had surprised her to realize she *hadn't* missed Doug. And if she hadn't missed him, why bother seeing him again? Why not just sever the relationship?

Aren't you just using him?

The question was sobering. Grace had never thought of their relationship in that way. Now that she had, she realized she *was* using him. But he was using her, too. Wasn't that the true nature of no-commitment relationships? Each party took what they wanted, and there were no deep emotions involved. There were also no regrets when the relationship dissolved.

Doug was convenient. He was charming, good-looking, successful and just as committed to his career as an investment adviser as she was to hers. He took her to nice places, they had fun together and they had terrific and energetic sex.

With no strings.

If Grace had to break a date or if she was too busy to see Doug, she never felt guilty. Nor did she hold it against him if he were too busy to see *her*.

So why was she even *thinking* of breaking it off?

Grace had just taken another sip of her hot chocolate and was beginning to realize she was hungry when she heard Emily crying. When, after five minutes, the crying got louder, she decided maybe she'd better get up and go check on Perry.

Although she was trying to be supportive, especially in view of Perry's depression, anger tightened Grace's jaw when she opened the door of the spare room. An unmoving Perry was buried under the covers. She had to have heard the baby. How could she not? Emily was crying in earnest now and she was less than five feet away.

"Shh," Grace said, going over to the bassinet and picking up the baby. "Well, no wonder you're crying," she said softly, cradling Emily in her arms. "You're soaking wet." Eyeing the bed, Grace was tempted to switch on the overhead light and force Perry to get up, but she changed her mind. What was the use? It would be quicker and simpler just to change and feed Emily herself. Grabbing a diaper from the pile stacked on a nearby chest, a fresh footie and the container of baby powder, Grace carried Emily across the hall to her bedroom. Soon Emily was dry and warm.

An hour later, with Emily happily full and lying contentedly in her carrier, Grace fixed herself a tuna-salad sandwich and another cup of hot chocolate and wondered if she should wake Perry.

She decided to let her sleep. Maybe then she'd get up for Emily's two o'clock feeding tonight, and Grace could get a full night's sleep. She had just settled back to enjoy the temporary quiet and had taken a bite of her tuna sandwich when the phone rang again. Snatching it up so as not to upset the baby, whose eyes had fluttered shut, Grace said a quiet, "Hello?"

"Hey, Gracie, how are you?"

Grace smiled. This time it was Michael, her youngest brother, calling. Michael was an artist and lived in Santa Fe with his girlfriend, Deanna, who was also an artist. Last year, they'd purchased a small gallery. "Hello, little brother. I'm fine. What about you?"

"I'm *great!*"

Grace's smile expanded. Michael had an exuberant personality. Nothing was ever good, it was always great. "And Deanna? Is she great, too?"

"She's fantastic."

Grace chuckled.

His voice sobered. "How's Perry doing?"

Grace put her sandwich down. Keeping her voice low, she gave Michael a rundown on the past few days.

"I think it's a good idea to have hired a nurse," he said when she'd finished. "Do you need help with the expense?"

Grace knew Michael and Deanna were struggling a bit financially, for the purchase of the gallery had strained their resources. "Thanks, but I can manage."

"You sure? It doesn't seem fair that you always have to do everything where she's concerned."

"I'm the one who said she could stay here."

"Yeah, but you knew Sal wouldn't want her with him, and Deanna and I couldn't take her."

"I really appreciate you offering," Grace said softly. "It means a lot to me."

They talked awhile more, and when Grace hung up, she felt better. Things were looking up. Maybe she'd been right to begin with. Maybe everything really *would* be all right.

"Don?"

"Yeah?"

"It's me. Perry." Perry was talking in a low tone so that Ingrid, the baby nurse Grace had hired to help her, wouldn't hear.

"Hey, babe, how's it going? Where are you? You had that kid yet?"

Tears filled Perry's eyes. She swallowed. "Y-yes, I had a

little girl. On Friday." Today was Wednesday. Emily was now five days old.

"Bet you're glad that's over."

"Yeah."

"So you're still in New York, huh?"

"Uh huh. I'm staying at my sister's."

"Man, I'm glad it's you and not me. I saw New York got eight inches of snow yesterday. Here, we just got sunshine. I couldn't live in the snow belt no more. You plannin' to stay there?"

"I don't want to," Perry whispered.

"I can't hear you, babe. You'll have to talk louder."

The tears that had threatened now spilled over. "I miss you, Don."

"Yeah, well, I miss you, too."

But Perry heard voices in the background. Was there already someone else? Was he just saying he missed her? She brushed away her tears. *Stop crying. Men hate when women cry.* "Are…are you still planning to move to Vegas?"

"Yep. Leavin' next week. Why don't you come with me, babe?"

Perry's heart leaped with hope. Maybe he really *did* miss her. "You mean, me and the baby?"

It was a moment before he answered. "Hey, look, I got nothin' against babies, but I told you before, I'm not raisin' some other guy's kid. I didn't change my mind about that."

"Oh."

"I'm sorry, but that's just the way it is."

"I'm sorry, too."

After that, there wasn't much to say, and soon Don said he had to go, that a couple of the guys were waiting, they were going to a neighborhood ice house to down a few beers and watch some big-screen TV. After the call was disconnected, Perry sat biting her lip and trying not to cry again. She was trembling with a sense of hopelessness that felt as if someone had scooped out her insides and left it empty.

Just then, the nurse walked into the living room. She gave Perry a searching look. "Is something wrong?"

Perry shook her head. "No, I'm fine."

"Are you sure? You look upset."

"It's nothing. I—I just talked to a friend and got a little homesick."

"Well, if you're okay, it's time to bathe Emily." She frowned when Perry didn't move. "C'mon. You're going to give her the bath. I'm just going to watch."

Perry wanted nothing more than to curl up on the couch and close her eyes but she couldn't stand the way Ingrid would look at her if she said so. Ingrid was kind, but she was also a no-nonsense type of person who thought all a person had to do to feel better was comb her hair and put on some lipstick and the rest would take care of itself. She'd probably never been depressed or unhappy a day in her life. She'd probably gotten straight As in school and had memorized all the multiplication tables before she was told she had to. Perry hated people like Ingrid.

And Grace.

At the thought, Perry felt sick. She didn't really hate Grace. She loved her. Grace was the best person she knew. In fact, Perry wasn't sure what she would do without Grace. It was just that Grace was so damned perfect.

And Perry was the world's biggest loser.

"All right, Ingrid," she said wearily. "I'm coming."

Grace lay pinned under the weight of Doug's arm. She was uncomfortable and wanted to turn on her side, but she didn't want to wake him. Sometimes, if he awakened in the night, he wanted to have sex again, and Grace wasn't in the mood. It wasn't that she hadn't enjoyed the sex tonight. She had. It had been great. Yet for some reason, tonight Grace had felt as if something were missing.

She sighed.

What was wrong with her?

She had the perfect life, the life she wanted, and still she wasn't satisfied. Tonight was a case in point. She and Doug had met at eight, had a wonderful dinner at the China Grill, where he'd been attentive and charming and entertaining. Then they'd come back here to his apartment where he'd put on a favorite Puccini CD, turned on the gas logs in his fireplace and poured them each a brandy.

Afterward, they'd gone to bed and, as usual, he'd been a skillful and knowledgeable lover. In fact, she'd had two orgasms.

So what else do you want?

A sign that he actually cared about her, maybe?

Sometimes Grace wondered if he ever gave her a thought during the day. Of course, then she felt guilty, because she rarely thought about *him* when she was at work.

Just then, Doug stirred and turned over, away from her. As quietly as possible, Grace eased herself out of bed. She wanted to go home but knew it would be crazy to go out and look for a cab at two in the morning. Instead, she grabbed one of the blankets stacked on the low chest at the foot the bed, wrapped it around herself, and tiptoed out to the living room where she stood in front of the sliding glass doors that led out to Doug's twenty-sixth-floor balcony.

The lights of the city were spread before her. Doug's apartment faced northeast and she could clearly see many of the city's landmarks: the Empire State Building, the Chrysler Building, Grand Central Terminal, even Rocke-feller Center. At this time of night, the city looked magical—the dirt and grime so visible during the day hidden now. Far below, sirens wailed in the distance.

The city that never sleeps…

When Grace was a child, she'd wanted to be a doctor. She'd had some romantic notion about working in the emergency room at night when everyone else was sleeping. Then she'd gotten older and decided that since she couldn't stand the sight of blood, being a doctor might not be such a great idea.

Her father had been thrilled when she'd settled on the legal profession. She'd known he would be. Maybe knowing how much it would please him if she became a lawyer had been the main reason she'd chosen the field. But she'd quickly realized she was eminently suited for it. She loved the way all the rules were there, you just had to look for them. She loved matching wits with other lawyers. And she especially loved the drama of the courtroom. *At heart, I'm probably a frustrated actress....*

"What're you doing out here?"

Grace jumped. "Oh, God," she said, putting her hand over her heart. "You startled me."

Doug walked up behind her and pulled her into his arms. "Come back to bed." He nuzzled her ear, his breath warm.

Grace shivered in his embrace.

"Come on. It's cold out here."

But she wasn't shivering because she was cold. She'd suddenly had that feeling her mother used to call *someone walking over my grave*.

"All right," she said reluctantly.

More than ever, all she wanted was to go home. She didn't even care that her apartment was no longer hers, that it was overrun with Perry's things, that it smelled of baby powder and soiled diapers, that the refrigerator was stuffed with bottles and the countertops in the kitchen were covered with baby paraphernalia.

Grace just knew she didn't belong here, in Doug's apartment. With Doug.

Maybe she never had.

Maybe Perry had actually done her a favor by coming

to stay with her. Because her presence in Grace's life had pointed up the complete absence of depth in her relationship with Doug. Hell, they weren't even *friends*.

In fact, she wasn't sure she even liked him.

And that was the saddest realization of all.

You should never look down on a sister except to pick her up.

—*Author Unknown*

CHAPTER 5

Grace trudged up Fifth Avenue and wished she'd taken a cab. February was her least favorite month, and this February was proving no exception. Dirty snow, freezing wind and treacherous pockets of ice made her progress difficult. She'd been conferring with a client whose offices were in Citibank and now she was on her way back to her office at Madison and Forty-fourth.

Well, she was on her way—but she decided a little detour to Lord and Taylor wouldn't be too time-consuming. Grace glanced in the window and saw a pair of black leather, fur-lined boots—ones she'd been coveting since winter had started. She almost went inside to give them a closer look, then sighed. Her bank balance still hadn't recovered from the private-duty nurse she'd hired to help Perry. She'd have to do with her old boots until she built up her reserves. Grace still remembered her student days and how difficult it had been to finally rid herself of debt. Now she did not believe in using credit cards for anything that wasn't essential.

Besides, all she really wanted right now was to get back to the office where it was warm and relatively peaceful and stay there. Although Emily was six weeks old now, and Perry had had help for more than a month after she'd been born, things still remained chaotic at home.

Perry was a terrible mother. She seemed not to have learned anything from the nurse and was still totally incapable of caring for Emily in any normal kind of way. Grace never knew what she'd find when she arrived home at night. Most evenings, she walked into an apartment that was a mess. Emily was usually crying, wet or hungry, and Perry—still wearing her ratty old bathrobe—was asleep on the couch with the television set blaring away.

The medication prescribed for Perry's depression wasn't helping. Of course, Grace couldn't be sure Perry was even taking it. For all she knew, her sister was flushing the pills down the toilet. The truth was, Grace wouldn't be surprised by anything Perry did or didn't do.

Grace was at her wit's end. The situation had gotten so bad, and she was so frustrated, she'd even called her brother Sal the other night.

He'd shown her little sympathy. "I told you the last time you bailed Perry out of a jam that you should have learned your lesson by now," he'd said. "Personally, I'd give her a deadline, say, two weeks. Then tell her she'll have to go."

"But Sal, she doesn't *have* any place to go...*or* any money," Grace protested. "Do you really think I should turn her *and the baby* out in the street?"

"Is that why you called? Because you want money?"

"No! This isn't about money. I just thought...oh, hell, never mind. I should have known better than to expect you to sympathize," she said tiredly.

"Look, Grace..." His voice softened. "I'm sorry. I know you think I'm a hard-hearted SOB, but I don't know what you want from me. I can't make Perry be different. We've all tried to help her over the years, but nothing ever changes. *She* never changes. And frankly, I've got problems of my own."

"What's wrong?" When he didn't immediately answer, she said, "Sal? Tell me. What is it?"

"Jen found a lump in her right breast."

Grace swallowed. "Oh, no. Has she seen her doctor?"

"Yeah. They're doing a biopsy tomorrow."

"Why didn't you call me?"

"Jen didn't want me to. Maybe it's nothing."

Grace nodded. For a long moment, neither of them spoke. "When will she know?"

"The doc said they'd have a pretty good idea as soon as they see the tissue, but they'll send it off for analysis to be sure. A couple of days, I guess."

"Maybe it *is* nothing."

"Maybe."

Grace knew he was thinking the same thing she was thinking. Jen had had a malignant lump in her left breast four years ago. She'd had a lumpectomy and chemo and all her follow-up CT scans had shown no trace of cancer.

But now…what if it was back?

Thinking about Jen and Sal, Grace knew her problems and even Perry's problems were minor in comparison. And yet, she also knew she was going to have to make some decisions about Perry soon. Because she was making no progress at all, and things could not continue the way they were.

By now Grace had reached her building and gratefully entered. When she walked into her secretary's office a few minutes later, Jamie gave her an odd look.

"What?" Grace said. She was already heading for the door leading to her own office.

"Grace, wait…"

But Grace had opened the door. Her mouth fell open, for sitting in the middle of her desk was a baby carrier, and inside, sleeping peacefully, was Emily.

Whirling around, she said, "What's going on?"

"I'm sorry, Grace. I tried to tell you. Your sister came by earlier and…she left the baby."

"Left the baby! What does she think we're running here? A babysitting service?" Her voice trembled, she was so angry. "Where the *hell* did she go?"

"Sh-she left you a note." Jamie backed away as if she thought Grace might strike her.

Calm down, calm down.... This isn't Jamie's fault. She's just the messenger....

Grace forced herself to take a deep breath. She snatched the note from Jamie and ripped open the envelope.

I'm sorry, Grace. I can't do this. Emily will be better off with you. I've talked to Don again, and he still wants me, so I'm going to meet him in L.A. I'll call you when we get settled. Please don't be mad. You'll be a great mother, I know you will. Emily already loves you. I left her birth certificate on your desk. I thought you might need it. Thank you for everything.
Love, Perry

Grace couldn't believe what she was reading. Her thoughts reeled. Perry was gone? Back to California? And she'd left Emily?

You'll be a great mother, I know you will....

Omigod.

What am I going to do?

I can't be a mother! I can't take care of a baby.

She looked at Jamie. "Does anyone else know the baby's here?" she whispered. Shock seemed to have stolen her voice.

Jamie shook her head. "No. Since she was sleeping I figured I'd just put her in here. If she'd started crying, I might have had to explain, but she didn't. She didn't even wake up. I've been checking on her every five minutes since your sister left."

Grace swallowed, then cleared her throat. *Think.* *Think.* "Did Perry even leave a bottle for her?"

"Yes, it's in the diaper bag." She inclined her head, and Grace saw the bag sitting on the credenza. "It was really cold," Jamie continued, "so I didn't think it needed to be refrigerated. Besides, if I'd taken it to the kitchen and put it in the fridge, I'd've had to explain why."

"Thank you, Jamie." Grace took off her coat and boots, her mind working furiously. What was she going to do? What the *hell* was she going to do?

"What's going on, Grace?"

Wordlessly, Grace handed Jamie the note.

Jamie's eyes rounded as she read. "Oh, boy," she said, looking up.

Grace bit her lip. Her gaze was drawn to Emily, who slept on, oblivious to the fact her mother had abandoned her. Grace's heart twisted as she studied the baby's sweet, innocent face. How could Perry have just left her like this? It was true that Grace had never wanted children— at least not after losing Brett—but she knew that if she *had* had a child, she never would have been able to do what Perry had done. The thing that puzzled her the most was why Perry had resisted placing Emily for adoption if, in the end, she was just going to walk away from her, anyway?

"What will you do?" Jamie asked softly.

"I don't know. I can hardly think." Grace walked over to her desk and lifted the carrier, gently placing it on the carpet. Emily made a squeaky sound, and her eyelashes—

dark and thick like her mother's—fluttered, but she quickly settled back into sleep.

Grace watched her for another long moment, then sighed and reached for her calendar. She was supposed to meet with Bill Madison, another of the junior partners, about the Finch lawsuit this afternoon, and tomorrow morning she had a deposition. Plus, she was scheduled to prep Marilyn Thomason for her court appearance next Monday. Dammit, anyway. And she had a lunch date set up with Lisa Rawley. Lisa Rawley was an eighteen-year-old former child actress who was suing her father for mismanagement of her money.

Grace's head hurt. *Think,* she told herself again. "Is Wallace in this afternoon?" she finally asked.

Jamie nodded. "I think so. I saw him walk down the hall about an hour ago."

"Please keep an eye on Emily. If she wakes up and starts to fuss, would you mind feeding her?"

"No, of course not."

"Thanks, Jamie. I'll owe you one. I'm going to go talk to Wallace."

"All right. Good luck."

Grace grimaced. "I'll need it."

Wallace Finn listened quietly as Grace explained her dilemma. "What would you like to do?" he asked when she'd finished.

Grace sighed. "I'd like to take three or four days of

vacation. Hopefully, that'll give me enough time to find good child care for the baby. After that, I don't know. I can't seem to think right now."

"Well, you certainly deserve some vacation. You haven't taken any in over two years. What's your calendar look like?"

"It's full, but I think I can reschedule just about everything."

Wallace nodded. "Anything that can't be rescheduled, give to Jack to take care of."

Grace kept her expression neutral. "I will."

They talked a few more minutes, then Grace thanked him and rose to leave.

"I'll come with you," he said, rising, too. "I'd like to see the baby."

Grace didn't know why she was surprised. Wallace had four grandchildren he adored. Their photographs were all over his office. "All right."

Later, as he stood gazing down at Emily, he said, "She's a beauty, Grace."

"Yes." Love constricted her heart—funny how this kid had wormed her way in—and once again Grace wondered how Perry could have left.

"If you need help finding someone to care for her, maybe Lucille can help." Lucille was his wife.

"Thank you. I'll remember that."

After he'd gone, Grace gave Jamie a list of instructions, then made a few quick phone calls. Just as Emily began to stir and make waking-up noises, Grace stuffed as much as she could into her briefcase and made preparations to leave.

"Okay, kid," she said softly, checking Emily to make sure she didn't need changing. "From now on, it's just you and me against the world."

Franklin gave Grace a curious look when she entered the foyer of her apartment building. She wondered what he was thinking. Deciding she didn't have to explain anything to him, she just smiled and waved and headed straight to the elevator.

The panic she'd felt in the office had faded. Now she was just angry. This escapade of Perry's was the last straw. Grace didn't care how depressed or overwhelmed Perry was, she had no business abandoning her baby. At the very least, she should have talked to Grace first, told her what she wanted to do. Of course, she probably knew if she *had*, Grace would have given her an unqualified *no*.

Once Grace had fed and changed Emily, she put her in her infant seat, placed it in the middle of the coffee table. "Be right back," she told the baby, then she hurried into her bedroom and found an envelope on her desk. Looking inside, she saw it contained the promised birth certificate.

Scanning it quickly, she saw that Perry had entered *father unknown* in the space provided for the father's name. That wasn't technically true, yet she could see why Perry had said so since she didn't know the guy's last name. And the truth was, saying the father was unknown would make things easier for Grace. Now, no matter what she might want to do in the future, she wouldn't have to worry about possible ramifications from that quarter.

She put the birth certificate inside the desk where it would be safe, then brought the phone and the Yellow Pages into the living room so she could keep an eye on Emily while she made her calls.

Deciding to take Wallace Finn's advice, she phoned his wife first. Lucille Finn was a lovely, motherly sort of woman, and she listened sympathetically as Grace explained the situation.

"Give me your number, Grace. I'll call Madeline, then phone you back." Madeline was the Finns' oldest daughter.

Grace made herself a cup of tea while she waited for Lucille's call. Emily lay contentedly in her infant seat, her eyes fastening on Grace when she walked back into the living room.

Grace smiled at the baby. "Hey," she said softly. Emily's eyes were a beautiful, clear slate-blue. She must have gotten both her dimples and eye color from her father, because no one in the Campisi family had blue eyes. Grace's father's eyes had been dark brown; Stella's were green. Reminded of her mother, Grace wondered if she should call and tell her what had happened. Stella had called the other night and talked to both Grace and Perry, so she knew Perry wasn't doing well. Still Grace hesitated. Stella would need to know Perry was gone, but Grace wanted to wait until she had some concrete plan in place before calling. Her mother would be very upset. She'd probably end up by blaming Grace. *But this isn't my fault....*

Just then, the phone rang. It was Lucille calling back. "Madeline found her nanny through this agency," Lucille said, then gave her the name and number of the agency. "She says they came highly recommended and that all their nannies and housekeepers are bonded and have passed a rigid background check."

"Thank you, Lucille. I really appreciate this."

An hour later, Grace had appointments to interview three different nannies. The woman she'd talked with had been frank with her, though. "You may have a hard time hiring someone," she'd warned. "Most of our nannies won't want to work the hours you're suggesting, not unless you're willing to pay *extremely* well."

Grace knew the woman was right. Six to eight would be a very long day. *Maybe I can cut my office hours a little, maybe leave the office at six and just bring work home....* She thought about how Jack Townsend stayed until eight every night, the same way she had before this mess with Perry had begun. How he came in most Saturdays and sometimes on Sundays.

Thinking about the partnership she wanted so badly, Grace felt sick. How could she do this? How could she be a mother to Emily and continue to be the kind of lawyer the firm would want at the partnership level?

Once again, Grace's eyes were drawn to the baby. Emily was kicking her feet, her attention captured by some reflection in the window. She'd filled out since her birth, and now, at six weeks, she weighed over ten pounds. A perfect baby, Grace thought. The kind of baby anyone would want....

Maybe I should place her for adoption. Wouldn't that be the best thing for her? To have two parents who really want a baby? I'm sure I wouldn't have any problem doing it once the court knew her mother had abandoned her....

Now Emily was waving her little arms in the air and making cooing sounds. She was so innocent. So helpless and dependent on Grace for everything, especially to make the right decisions for her. Suddenly Grace understood a little of how overwhelmed Perry must have felt. It was frightening to realize that you were totally responsible for someone else, and must have been even more frightening for Perry, who had never even been able to take care of herself.

Grace reached over and touched Emily's hand. The baby immediately latched on to her forefinger, her gaze swinging to meet Grace's. Then, in a stunning moment Grace knew she'd never forget, Emily smiled. It was her first real smile; the others had appeared quickly, when she'd been half-asleep.

Grace's heart contracted, love filling her. And she made a solemn vow. "I'll do my very best for you, sweetheart," she promised. "Whatever it takes, I won't let you down."

A sister is both your mirror and your opposite.
—*Elizabeth Fishel*

CHAPTER 6

"I wish I could say yes, Ms. Campisi, but I'm taking classes at NYU at night, so I would have to be able to leave here no later than six." The speaker, Alexis Woodward, was a beautiful blond girl in her early twenties. She gave Grace an apologetic smile.

Alexis was the third young woman Grace had interviewed, and she was by far the most desirable. She had this cheerful, upbeat kind of personality, and it was obvious from her speech patterns and vocabulary that she was well-educated and intelligent. Grace liked the way she talked about Emily and the way she smiled at the baby, saying, "Oh, she's adorable. Look at those dimples!" And most importantly, Alexis's references were impeccable.

"You don't have classes every night, do you?" Grace asked.

Alexis shook her head. "No, just Tuesdays and Thursdays."

"Well, how would it be if I promised to be home by five-thirty on those nights, but you stayed until seven-thirty the other three nights?"

"Friday, too?" A slight frown had appeared.

"I'll be home by six on Fridays," Grace said. The compromise would still impact her job, but not as badly as it could have.

"That could work," Alexis said slowly.

"How about if we have a trial period? Say a month. If you're unhappy or I'm unhappy by the end of the month, we can just call it quits with no hard feelings." What Grace would do then, she had no idea, but right now she just needed to know that the immediate future would be taken care of. That *Emily* would be taken care of. Maybe by the end of a month, Grace would have heard from Perry.

"All right. That sounds fair."

They agreed that Alexis would begin the next morning. Grace decided she would still take the day off to make sure Alexis was comfortable with Emily. Grace also needed to make some purchases, like a proper crib for the baby, a changing table and a small chest to hold Emily's clothing and supplies. Because she hadn't expected Perry to stay long, they'd made do with a bassinet and putting a waterproof pad on Perry's bed when the baby's diaper needed to be changed.

After Alexis left, Grace let out a whoosh of relief. Her new nanny was going to cost her dearly—in fact, Grace needed to take a long, hard look at her finances to see where she might cut—but it would be worth it to have reliable care for Emily. Well worth it. And once she was made a partner—she was determined to think positive!—she would be given a hefty boost in salary as well as a share of the profits at the end of the year, which would be considerably more than her current year-end bonus.

So Alexis's salary was more than just the cost of good child care. It was also an investment in Grace's future. A future that was even more important now than it had been yesterday.

"I just can't believe it."

"Believe it, Mom," Grace said. She and her mother had been talking for more than thirty minutes, and Stella still couldn't seem to accept the fact that Perry had abandoned her baby.

"She wasn't thinking straight, you know she wasn't. Perry would never do something like that if she had been," her mother said for at least the third time.

Grace sighed. "It doesn't matter whether she was thinking straight or not, does it? The outcome is still the same. She dumped her baby."

"She'll be back. Once she realizes what she's given up, she'll come back."

Grace wished she could believe that. The trouble was, Perry had always run away from her problems. Why should this time be any different? "Well, I just wanted to let you know what happened. I'd better go now. I hear Emily stirring. She'll be hungry."

"Oh, okay."

"I'll call you if I hear from Perry."

Emily hadn't really stirred. Grace had just wanted to get off the phone because the conversation with her mother wasn't going anywhere but in circles.

Why did her mother always defend Perry and make excuses for her? Couldn't she, just once, admit to Grace that Perry was totally irresponsible, that she'd screwed up big time? It was almost as if, by admitting Perry's weaknesses, Stella would be betraying her.

That never stopped her where I'm *concerned,* Grace thought with a resentment that sometimes overshadowed her love for her mother.

Rubbing her head—she had the beginnings of a headache, something that almost always happened when she talked to her mother—Grace stared out her living-room window. She knew that soon she would have to make some hard decisions, like whether she would keep and raise Emily herself, as Perry had assumed, or whether she would investigate adoption possibilities.

For some reason, the thought of giving the baby away caused an ache in her chest, even though, before she'd been born, it was what Grace had believed would be best for Emily. *But that was before I knew her. Before I came to love her.* She guessed that was why she had been so shocked by Perry's abandonment. Because surely Perry had come to love her child, too.

Grace laid her forehead against the cool glass and closed

her eyes. Although she'd long since strayed from the religion of her youth, she whispered, "Please, Holy Mother, help me do the right thing...."

Her prayer was interrupted by Emily's cry.

As Grace hurried to tend to the baby, she decided she was not going to worry about the future. For now, she'd simply take things one day at a time.

Grace looked at the stack of files on her desk, every one of which needed her attention yesterday. Her day had been a bitch, and it wasn't over yet. She still needed to read through the research material her paralegal had prepared for the Rawley case, and it was almost five o'clock. *Damn*. Alexis had class tonight. If Grace was going to make it home by five-thirty, she'd have to leave right now. And pray she could find a cab.

She reached for her briefcase and shoved the report inside, then grabbed several other documents that needed her attention. She had just put on her coat and boots when there was a knock on her door. "Yes?" she called, thinking it was Jamie saying goodbye.

The door swung open and Skip Foster walked in. Skip was another junior partner angling for a senior partnership, but Grace wasn't worried about him because she didn't think he had much of a chance.

"You leaving?" he asked. "Already?" His expression was exaggeratedly incredulous.

Grace felt like giving him the finger. Instead, she smiled sweetly and said, "Did you need something, Skip?"

"Neil Braddock has called a meeting to go over the Eagleton case. He wants everyone in the small conference room at five-thirty."

Oh, shit. The last thing Grace wanted to do was miss out on anything to do with the Eagleton Energy case, which was a class-action lawsuit by a group of former female employees of the energy company. They were accusing Eagleton management of discrimination and abuse of power. Grace's firm was representing the company. It was an important case with powerful ramifications should the company lose. Neil Braddock— second only to Wallace Finn in the firm—was handling the defense of Eagleton himself, with Grace sitting second chair.

"Thank you," she said. When Skip still stood there, she gave him a pointed look.

Taking the hint, he shrugged and walked out. She shut the door behind him. Removing her coat, she hung it back up, then walked over to her desk where she picked up the phone.

"Alexis?" she said when the girl answered.

"Oh, hello, Ms. Campisi."

"Look, Alexis, I know I said I'd be there by five-thirty, but something urgent has come up, and I'm not going to be able to make it."

Silence greeted this announcement.

"I'm so sorry," Grace hurriedly added. "I feel terrible about this, but it can't be helped. I'll make it up to you, I promise."

"When *will* you be home?"

Grace winced at the icy tone. "I don't know," she admitted. "No later than eight o'clock. Is...will that be okay?"

"I guess it will have to be, won't it?"

Throughout the meeting, Grace kept thinking about Alexis and the coldness in her voice during their phone conversation. Grace felt bad. She knew it wasn't fair to have promised the girl something, then reneged on that promise in the first week of her employ. But what could Grace have done? She couldn't jeopardize her position as second chair on this case. It was too important. It wouldn't kill Alexis to miss one class, she rationalized, and Grace would pay her handsomely to make up for it.

Luckily, the meeting was over at seven-fifteen, and Grace breathed a sigh of relief. She would have hated to be later than the eight she'd promised.

She had repacked her briefcase and was just on her way out of the conference room to get her coat and take off for home when Neil Braddock put a hand on her arm, saying, "Grace, wait. Don't rush off. I was thinking I'd buy you dinner so we can discuss strategy."

"Oh, Neil, I'm sorry, but I have to get home."

He frowned, his steely-blue eyes narrowing. "Oh?"

Damn, damn, damn. No one ever said no to Neil

Braddock, not if they hoped to keep in his good graces. "I really am sorry," she said again. "I don't know if Wallace told you or not, but I've got…temporary custody of my sister's baby, and I promised the sitter I wouldn't be any later than eight o'clock."

"I see."

So Wallace Finn *hadn't* told him.

"Well, that's unfortunate," he said, brushing an imaginary piece of lint off his dark gray suit.

She wondered if he meant it was unfortunate she couldn't go tonight or if having the baby itself was unfortunate. Probably both. "Could we meet tomorrow morning?"

"I have a full schedule tomorrow," he replied coolly. "It will have to wait until next week."

Oh, great. She could see how pissed he was and knew this black mark wouldn't be forgotten anytime soon. So now she had three people angry with her, because Doug had called earlier wanting to take her to dinner—in other words, he wanted sex—and she'd had to say no to him, too. *I'm dancing as fast as I can*, she cried inwardly.

Doug's reaction didn't bother her. She'd pretty much made up her mind to break things off with him. But Alexis and Neil Braddock were both important. Unfortunately, appeasing one meant antagonizing the other, and Grace had a sinking feeling this wouldn't be the last time she'd have to choose between them.

By the time she reached her apartment, she felt both mentally and physically exhausted, and her head was pounding. Seeing Alexis's stony face when she walked inside didn't help.

"I'm so sorry," Grace said. When Alexis's expression didn't change, Grace wondered what the girl wanted her to do. Fall prostrate at her feet?

"I just want you to know, Ms. Campisi, that if this happens again, you will have to find someone else to watch Emily."

Grace nodded. She was too tired to argue or plead. Digging in her purse, she pulled out her wallet and extracted a fifty-dollar bill. "Here," she said. "I hope this helps make up for missing your class."

"Thank you." Alexis took the bill. "Emily is asleep. I gave her a bath and fed her at seven. She should sleep until her two o'clock feeding. I'll see you in the morning."

Five minutes later she was gone.

Grace wearily removed her coat and tossed it on the sofa. Putting her briefcase on the coffee table, she toed off her boots—not even caring that they were probably wet and might dirty the carpet—then quietly walked to the door of the former spare room. The door was slightly open, and she pushed it in gently, then tiptoed inside. She stood at the crib and looked down at the baby, who lay on her back, her mouth slightly open. The mobile above the crib swayed faintly in the air current from the heating vent. Grace leaned over and gently kissed Emily's forehead, breathing in the mingled scents of baby powder and milk. A fierce love gripped her. "I'll figure this out somehow," she whispered.

Emily's body twitched in that way Grace was coming to recognize as something infants do in sleep. Grace's stomach rumbled—she'd skipped lunch—but even though she was hungry and tired and couldn't wait to sink down into a comfortable chair and put her feet up, she couldn't seem to make herself move. For the first time in her life, she truly understood the enormity of the responsibility of having a child.

Can I do this?

Grace didn't know.

She only knew she had to try.

For the next week, there were no emergencies at work, and no crises at home. Still, Grace was on tenterhooks. She knew things wouldn't remain on this even keel. Sure enough, just eight days after Alexis's ultimatum, Neil Braddock again asked Grace to stay late and have dinner with him so they could go over strategic points in the Eagleton case. Just the way he issued the invitation told Grace this was a test, and she'd better pass it this time.

"I'd be happy to," she said. Thank God this was not one of Alexis's school nights. Praying the girl wouldn't be upset, Grace hurried back to her office to call home.

"I'm sorry, Ms. Campisi, but I can't stay late tonight," Alexis said. "I have a date."

"Alexis, when you took this job, you knew I might have an occasional emergency."

"Yes, but you've been late every single night since I started."

"Not *that* late," Grace said. "Except for that one night when I called you, I've never been more than thirty minutes past the time I said I'd be."

"You caused me to be late for class on Thursday and to miss my train on Friday."

"Please, Alexis, I'm begging you. I have to have dinner with my boss tonight. I have to. I told him no the last time he asked, and I just can't go in and tell him no again. Can't you break your date?" In desperation, Grace added, "Tell your date to come to the apartment. Order take-out Chinese or something. And I'll get there just as soon as I can."

Alexis's sigh was audible. "This is the first time I'm going out with this guy. I'm not inviting him to your apartment. I don't know him well enough to do that." Her voice softened. "Look, Ms. Campisi, I'm sorry for you. I know you're having a tough time. But this just isn't going to work out for me. You're going to have to find someone else. What I recommend is a live-in."

Grace closed her eyes. *Oh, God...* "Please don't leave, Alexis. Please give me some time to figure things out. I— I'm so new at this."

"I know you are, and I really am so sorry. Frankly, I'd hate to be in your position, but I can't take on your problems. I have my own life to lead. Part of this is my fault, I know. I never should have taken this job, but I was so enchanted with Emily that I let that cloud my better judgment. She really is such a sweetheart."

Grace swallowed. "Yes."

"Look," Alexis said. "I'll cancel my date for tonight. But you have to find someone else. Two weeks from now, I'm leaving."

"Miss Campisi, I don't know how you think you're going to hire a live-in. A live-in requires a room of her own."

"But I only *have* two bedrooms," Grace said to the woman at the agency specializing in live-in help. "Couldn't she share with the baby?"

"No, that's out of the question. I wouldn't even *ask* one of my nannies to do such a thing, because I know what the answer would be."

Grace's thoughts whirled around in her head like a tornado. What to do, what to do, what to do...

She thought about moving, buying a bigger apartment, but how? She'd stretched her finances as far as she reasonably could to buy *this* apartment, and even though it had already increased in value, so had the larger apartments. There was no way she could afford a bigger apartment, not unless she got the partnership, and then only after she received her share of the firm's profits in December.

Dear Lord, please help me. I don't know what I'm going to do.

No matter what she was doing at work or at home, the question was always in her mind throughout the next few days. Over and over she considered her options. It was at times like these she desperately wished for someone to talk to. Someone objective, someone who cared about her, someone who didn't have a stake in her decision.

A best friend.

But best friends—*any* friend, for that matter—required time, effort and commitment, things Grace lavished on her career with little left for anything else.

So when, three days after Alexis's ultimatum, Jamie said, "Grace, do you want to talk about it?" Grace nodded miserably.

"Want a cup of coffee first?" Jamie asked, her hazel eyes filled with sympathy.

"Yes, please."

Five minutes later, Grace's office door closed, steaming mugs of coffee in front of them, the two women talked. Grace told Jamie everything that had happened since the day Perry had left Emily at the office.

Jamie grimaced when Grace told her about Neil Braddock's reaction to her first refusal of dinner.

"Not good," she said.

"No," Grace said. She knew Jamie wanted her to get the partnership almost as badly as she wanted it herself, for Jamie's status—and salary—would go up right along with Grace's.

When Grace finished her recital of woes, Jamie gave her a thoughtful look. "Grace, have you thought about placing Emily for adoption?"

Grace sighed. "Yes."

"Did you know Bruce Standish and his wife are trying to adopt?"

"No, I didn't know that." Bruce was a senior partner, one of the nicest men in the firm and someone Grace admired.

"They'd be wonderful parents, don't you think?"

Grace nodded thoughtfully. They'd be *perfect* parents. In fact, Grace couldn't think of any two people who would be better qualified or could give a baby a better home. From the first time she'd seen them together as a couple, she'd been struck by what a good relationship they seemed to have. Emily would want for nothing if the Standishes adopted her. They had money, position, a strong marriage, a gorgeous home in Westchester County. And Margaret was a stay-at-home wife. *They're certainly better qualified and equipped to raise Emily than I am.... In fact, I'm a complete failure at this....*

Grace had never failed at anything she put her mind to. And the realization that she was failing now was sobering. She swallowed.

Maybe it was time to go talk to Bruce Standish.

Perry kept dreaming about Emily. In the dream, Emily was crying for her. Perry would wake up shaking and wanting to cry herself. Thank God Don was such a heavy sleeper. Otherwise, he'd probably be totally disgusted with her.

During the day, Perry knew her dreams were brought on by guilt. And she also knew that if Emily could talk, she'd say she liked being with Grace a whole lot better than she'd liked being with Perry.

And who could blame her? Grace wasn't a screwup like Perry. If she set her mind to something, she did it, and she did it perfectly. Who *wouldn't* prefer her to be their mother?

Maybe someday I'll have another little girl and I'll be able to keep her.

And in the meantime, her first little girl was in the best place she could ever be.

With her sister.

How do people make it through life without a sister?

—Sara Corpening

CHAPTER 7

Grace dreaded making the phone call. She'd put if off for days, but it had to be done. Taking a deep breath, she picked up the phone and pressed the speed-dial code for her mother.

"Hello?"

Grace smiled. "Hi, Aunt Mutt." Her mother's older sister's name was really Matilda, but she'd been called Mutt since she was a kid, probably because, when she and Grace's mom had been little, their younger brother couldn't pronounce Matilda.

"Oh, hello, Grace," her aunt said. "How are you doing, honey?"

"I'm hanging in there."

"Stella told me about Perry and the baby and everything. I can't imagine how you're managing, not with your job and all."

"I'm not," Grace said with a rueful laugh.

"This is so typical of Perry, isn't it?"

Their aunt didn't wear the same rose-colored glasses their mother wore when it came to Perry. "Yeah," Grace said. "I shouldn't have even been surprised when it happened."

"Well, I give you credit for everything you've done for your sister, even if she doesn't appreciate it."

Grace was surprised that her aunt would say such a thing, because it was bound to upset Grace's mother. "Um, is Mom there?"

"She went down for the mail."

Ah. That explained it.

"She'll be back any minute."

Grace and her aunt chatted another few minutes, then Mutt said brightly, "Here's your mom now, Grace. It was good talking to you. Come and see us soon, won't you?"

"I will. Bye, Aunt Mutt. I love you."

"And I love you, too, sweetie. Give that baby a kiss for me. And send us more pictures!" Grace made a mental note to buy herself a digital camera so she wouldn't have to mail photos and could instead load them onto the Net for her mother and aunt to see. *And Perry, too, if I ever hear from her again…*

A moment later, Grace's mother was on the phone. "Hi, Grace," she said. "I was going to call you tonight. Thanks for the pictures you sent of Emily. Oh, she's so beautiful. I can't wait to see her. Do you think you might be able to bring her down soon?"

"Mom…"

Something in Grace's tone must have alerted her mother, for her voice sharpened. "What?"

Grace took another deep breath. "Mom, there's a lawyer with my firm, a really wonderful man that I think highly of. He and his wife have been trying to adopt a baby for months, and I've…I've talked to him about adopting Emily."

"No!" her mother cried. "No, you can't *do* that, Grace. You can't!"

"I know this is a shock, but please try to understand. I work horrendous hours. I'm hardly ever home for Emily. My nanny has given me her notice because of those hours, and so far, I've had no luck finding someone to live in. And even if I did find someone who'd be willing to move into my apartment where she'd have no room of her own, what kind of life would that be for Emily? She'd be raised by a paid nanny. Asleep in the morning when I leave for work, asleep at night when I get home. I'd hardly ever see her. It's not fair to her. She deserves to live in a home with a mother and a father who adore her and will spend lots of time with her." Grace gulped some of the already-cooled coffee Jamie had placed on her desk earlier. "Don't you see? There's really no choice here. This is the right thing to do."

Now her mother was weeping. "Oh, if only I could take her," she sobbed. "What about Sal and Jennifer? Have you talked to them? Maybe they could do it."

"Mom, you know they can't. Their kids are grown. Jen has a job she loves." She thought about telling her mother about Jen's latest cancer scare, then decided against it. The lump had turned out to be benign. No sense upsetting her mother further.

"Have you asked him?"

"There's no point." Grace told her what Sal had told her the first time they'd discussed Perry's pregnancy.

"You know, Grace, not everyone feels the way you do about children. Does he know you have her now?"

Grace counted to ten. "Yes, he knows." She could've added that Sal hadn't even asked to see the baby. But that would be lowering herself to a level that was beneath her, because Grace understood why her brother didn't want to see the baby. Sal didn't want to get emotionally involved because he was afraid of risking his heart, and he knew he couldn't afford to. *Like I have…*

"Maybe Michael…"

"Michael and Deanna can't do it. They just bought the gallery. Finances are tight. It would be terribly unfair to put pressure on him to take Emily. I'm going to tell him what I plan, and if, by some chance, he should offer, then we'll talk about it. But I don't think he will."

"But Emily's your *niece*," her mother cried. "She's my *granddaughter!*"

"Don't you think I know that, Mom?" Grace said wearily. "I'm thinking of what's best for her."

"You're thinking of what's best for yourself! You could do this if you wanted to. You've done everything else you ever wanted to do."

Grace didn't know why her mother's accusation hurt so

much. She should be used to being portrayed as the bad guy. "If you choose to think of it that way, I can't stop you," she replied stiffly.

Although her mother apologized, their goodbye was strained, and Grace knew her mother would continue to believe that Grace was selfish, whereas nothing Perry ever did was her fault. Their mother would make excuses for Perry until the day she died.

No, Grace thought. *No. I'm not going there. Forget what Mom said. It's not important, and she'll never change. What's important is doing what you know is right.*

Her mind made up, Grace reached for the phone. She'd tell Bruce Standish to go ahead and get the ball rolling on his petition to adopt Emily.

"Have you tried to find Perry?" The question came from Michael, whom Grace had called when she'd gotten home that evening.

"I have no idea where to look. I don't know this Don's last name."

"What about your phone records? Didn't you say Perry had called him?"

"I thought of that, and I actually found a number listed that I didn't recognize."

"And?"

"It's no longer in service."

"Which means they've probably already moved wherever they're moving to."

Or he didn't pay the bill. "She said Vegas, but who knows? They could have changed their minds."

"For what it's worth," Michael said, "I think you're doing the right thing."

"Thanks. Mom doesn't."

"Oh, Mom. You know how she is. Perry's her *baby*."

"Yes, I know."

"Gracie, don't take anything she says to heart. She means well."

"Dammit, Michael, she *doesn't* mean well. She means to hurt me. She as much as said she thinks I'm selfish. But not Perry. Oh, no. Not Perry."

"Well, I don't think you're selfish, and neither does Sal. And I'm sure Perry doesn't, either. Mom's just... Mom. I'm surprised she hasn't called me to ask *me* to take the baby."

"She suggested it."

"Jeez, Grace, is that why you're calling? Were *you* planning to ask me? I mean, Deanna—"

"No, no. I just thought I should tell you what I'm doing. As Mom pointed out, Emily's our niece."

"Okay, I'm sorry."

Grace could hear the relief in his voice. She couldn't blame him. Why *should* he feel an obligation to raise Perry's baby? Why should any of them?

"How's that going to work?" he asked after a moment. "Letting that couple adopt Emily? I mean, since you're not the mother?"

"Perry abandoned her baby, Michael. The court won't look favorably on that."

"But won't they try to locate her?"

"Maybe. Maybe not. There's no hard and fast rule. It'll be up to the family-court judge, who has the power to terminate Perry's parental rights. Then Emily will be free to be adopted." Grace had thoroughly researched New York's adoption laws, as had Bruce Standish.

"What if Perry comes back after Emily's been adopted and wants her back?"

"That, too, would be up to the court. Frankly, I can't worry about it. I have to assume she's *not* coming back and do what I think is best."

"I know. I was just wondering, that's all."

They talked awhile more, then said their goodbyes. Afterward, Grace sat pensively. She knew she was doing the right thing, so why was it so hard?

And why did she keep second-guessing her decision?

Perry wished she could call Grace, but she was afraid to. She knew Grace must be pissed off big time. *I did the right thing, though. I know I did. Grace will take much better care of Emily than I ever could.* Thinking about Emily made Perry's stomach hurt. But it wasn't as if she wouldn't ever be able to see her again. Once Grace had had a few months to calm down, Perry could call her, then she could go and visit.

If Grace will let me. Maybe she'll tell Emily I'm a horrible person and she won't let her see me.

"Hey, babe, why so quiet?" Don looked over at her and frowned. "Aren't you excited?"

They were on their way to Vegas. Had left the motel where they'd been staying the past few days about ten o'clock that morning. Perry pushed thoughts of Emily and Grace to the back of her mind. Don didn't like it when she *moped around,* as he called it. She forced herself to smile brightly. "I was just thinking about Bud and Peggy. Are you sure they won't mind us staying with them?"

"How many times do I have to tell you? Bud said we can stay at their place as long as we need to."

"I wish we didn't have to stay with them." Perry didn't like Bud. She'd only met him once, but once was enough. He was loud and constantly told off-color jokes, mainly about women and their "hooters" and he had a beer belly that wouldn't quit. He and Don had gone to high school together.

"As soon as I find a job, we'll get our own place." Don reached over and squeezed her thigh. "Quit worryin', will you? It'll be fine."

"Just don't go off hitting the bars with him and leaving me home with Peggy."

Don laughed. "Is that what you're worried about?" His hand moved farther up her thigh, inching under her denim skirt. "I won't leave you," he said softly.

Perry's breath hitched as his fingers crept under her panties. "Don, stop."

"Why?" he said, grinning. "No one can see us. Anyway, you like it, don't tell me you don't."

Perry grabbed his hand and pushed it away. "No, I don't. Not here."

He sighed elaborately. "There's no pleasin' some women. First they want it. Then they don't. Fine. I won't touch you again."

Oh, shit. He was mad now. Perry couldn't stand it when he was mad at her. "Don, don't be that way. You know I always want you. Just not here, in broad daylight, where any trucker can come along and see what you're doing."

He drummed his fingers on the steering wheel of his Bronco. "I might just have to find me someone more willing. Someone who's not ashamed of me."

Perry hated when he did this. He knew she was crazy about him. Most of the time, all he had to do was look at her and she was ready. "Please, Don, don't be mad. You know how I feel about you. And I'd *never* be ashamed of you. I just don't want anyone to see us, because I think what we do together is private." She wanted to say *Besides, you're driving, and I don't want to end up in an accident*, but she knew better than to criticize him.

He didn't reply.

Now she reached over and touched his thigh. "Don?"

"What?"

"Please don't be mad."

He shrugged. "If you really loved me, you'd show me."

Perry bit her bottom lip.

"Seems to me you just want a meal ticket."

Perry's eyes filled with tears. "How can you say that?" She

swallowed, fighting for control. She knew he didn't mean what he'd said, that he was just pissed off because she'd denied him something he wanted, yet the remarks hurt.

"Oh, for Christ's sake," he said, looking at her now. "Will you turn off the waterworks?"

Perry knew if it had been her sister whose boyfriend had said the things Don had just said, Grace would have gotten pissed off right along with him. She'd have told him off. She certainly wouldn't have let him make her cry. But Perry wasn't strong like Grace. She might not have needed Don for a meal ticket, as he'd suggested, but she did need him. She needed him desperately, and she couldn't stand it when he was angry with her.

"I'm sorry," she said, brushing away her tears. She gave him a watery smile, then scooted over as close as she could. Reaching for the zipper to his jeans, she tugged at it until she could pull it down. Then she plunged her hand inside.

He didn't look at her, but the corners of his mouth lifted, and his voice was husky as he said, "Now you're cookin', babe. Yeah. Now you're cookin'."

Of two sisters, one is always the watcher, one the dancer.

—*Louise Glück*

CHAPTER 8

After much thought, Grace decided before any paperwork was filed or any petitions launched, it would be a good idea for her and Emily to pay a visit to Bruce and Margaret Standish. Bruce readily agreed.

"Margaret and I had the same idea, but I hated to be the one to bring it up," he said.

"Why?" Grace asked.

"I thought you might think we wanted to check out the goods first," he admitted, "and I didn't want to do anything to botch the deal."

Grace nodded. She could understand that. Especially in light of how important this decision was to all of them.

They decided that Grace should bring Emily and come to Sunday dinner that weekend.

"We'll send a car for you," Bruce said. "Would eleven

in the morning work for you? We'll plan on dinner about one and get the two of you back home before dark."

"Eleven is fine, but a car's not necessary. I can come up on the train."

"We'll send a car," he insisted.

Since Grace had never attempted to take the baby anywhere except for a couple of short trips in a cab, she didn't need much persuading. Every day her respect for mothers grew. How they managed with one, let alone two and three kids, was beyond her. Just the stuff that had to be carted along when you were going somewhere was daunting. She cringed when she remembered how superior she'd once felt to women who chose to stay at home with their children. How she'd believed their "work" wasn't really work at all, at least not on a par with her work at the firm. And she certainly hadn't had a clue about what mothers who also held outside jobs faced. Why, any woman who could manage a demanding career as well as the responsibilities of running a home and raising children should be paid on a par with CEOs. And *single* mothers…their responsibilities were staggering. They should all be declared saints. Grace shook her head remembering her offhand scorn. How *could* she have been so arrogant?

Sunday morning dawned sunny, windy and cold. It was now the third week of March and New Yorkers were tired of winter and longing for spring. But so far, the weather hadn't cooperated. As Grace dressed in black wool slacks and a white cable-knit sweater, then put Emily in equally warm clothes, she couldn't help thinking how much easier life was for people who lived in a warmer climate.

Since Bruce had said the car would arrive at eleven, Grace had planned to be downstairs in the lobby about ten minutes early so that the driver would not have to worry about finding a place to park, but just as she was ready to walk out the door, Franklin buzzed her to tell her the car and driver were there waiting.

Struggling to carry the infant seat, the full diaper bag and Emily, as well as her own handbag (she could see she was going to have to invest in some shoulder bags), Grace managed to get her apartment locked and herself and the baby and all their paraphernalia down to the lobby within five minutes of Franklin's call.

The car Bruce had sent was a luxurious Lincoln and the driver turned out to be a young man with a Brooklyn accent and a friendly smile. He grinned at Emily in her pink knitted sweater and cap, snugly wrapped in a white cashmere blanket. "What a cute baby. How old is she?"

When Grace said Emily was nine weeks old, he said, "I thought so. My niece is two months old and they look about the same size." Then he added, "My name is Pete, Miss Campisi."

"Hello, Pete."

He opened the back door for her and Grace was amazed to see an infant's rear-facing car seat.

"Mr. Standish said he figured you wouldn't have one," Pete said.

Grace hadn't even thought of one, but now that it was there, she belatedly realized the law required children to be protected when riding in cars. She thought about how she'd brought Emily home from the office the day Perry had left her and the day she'd taken her to the pediatrician. Both times they'd ridden in a cab and Grace had held the baby in her arms. What if they'd had an accident? Emily could have been badly hurt. It frightened Grace even to think about it. Oh, boy, she had a lot to learn. Why, she didn't even know how to buckle the baby in!

Pete said, "Here, let me. I've got experience with these things." He showed her how the restraints worked, and soon Emily was safely ensconced and Grace was buckled into her seat belt, and they were off.

Bruce and Margaret lived just past Dobbs Ferry, which was about an hour's drive, even considering she lived in lower Manhattan. Their route took them from the George Washington Bridge to the Henry Hudson Parkway and then to the Saw Mill Parkway. Grace enjoyed the beautiful scenery along the way. It was nice to look at something other than concrete. They passed some pretty river towns, and Emily—lulled by the motion of the car—fell asleep and slept throughout most of their trip.

Grace had been to the Standish home once before, for a summer barbecue to which all the associates had been invited. She remembered it as warm and inviting—the kind of place where you immediately felt comfortable.

As they drove through Dobbs Ferry, Grace wondered what it would be like to live there. It was a charming, historic town with a beautiful waterfront and dramatic views of the Hudson River.

The road the Standishes lived on was curved and slightly hilly. Their home stood at the top of a rise, where the road curved almost in a U. The back of the house had a stunning view of the river and Grace remembered how envious she'd been when she'd first seen it.

Pete pulled the car into the driveway and stopped at the front walk, which led to the entrance of the large brick Tudor home. He'd barely gotten out of the car and walked around to open Grace's door when the massive double entrance doors opened and Bruce Standish appeared.

It was odd to see him in khaki pants and a sweater instead of the elegantly tailored suits he wore in the office. In his mid-fifties, Bruce was handsome by anyone's standards with his salt-and-pepper hair, striking blue eyes, square jaw and charming smile.

He was beaming as Pete helped Grace out of the car, then unfastened the restraints holding Emily into the car seat. Bruce greeted Grace warmly, but his eyes were on Emily as Pete extracted her from the car. "What a beauty," he said softly.

Emily's eyes opened as Pete handed her to Grace, and she yawned, then stretched, screwing her face up as she did.

Bruce's eyes never left the baby's face. "She's incredible, Grace."

Grace was surprised at her reaction. She was proud of Emily and pleased that Bruce recognized how special the baby was, but overriding these two emotions was another, darker one. Her arms tightened around the baby, even though she instinctively knew Bruce wanted to hold her. An odd twinge of reluctance shot through her. *She's not yours yet.* The unworthiness of the thought shamed her. *What's wrong with you?*

Just then, Margaret Standish joined them. Grace hadn't even seen her approach. A petite woman with dark eyes and short auburn hair, she was about ten years younger than her husband. In her long wool skirt and cinnamon twin set, she could have passed for a woman in her thirties. She, too, had eyes only for Emily, although she greeted Grace graciously. "Oh," she said, tears shining in her eyes. "Oh, she's so beautiful." After a long moment, her eyes met Grace's. "May I hold her?"

Grace would have had to be the cruelest woman on earth to say anything but yes. But the moment she handed Emily over to Margaret, her arms felt bereft.

The tears in Margaret's eyes overflowed as she snuggled Emily close. She smiled through them. "Don't mind me, I'm terribly emotional."

Bruce gave his wife a tender smile. "She always cries when she's happy."

Grace, swallowing against the lump in her throat, nodded. She felt like crying herself.

"Why don't you two gals take Emily and go on inside

where it's warm?" Bruce said. "I'll settle up with Pete here and be in in a minute."

Walking inside the spacious foyer, Grace couldn't help but compare the Standish home with her own small, cluttered apartment. It was a showplace, with gleaming wood floors, richly colored Oriental carpets, a beautiful mix of antique and more modern, traditional furniture, fresh flowers and warm colors. Despite the richness of the furnishings and decorations, it was also welcoming—the kind of place you knew was truly lived in, where it wouldn't be out of place to see children running around or a cat sitting on the windowsill. The thought had no sooner crossed Grace's mind when a beautiful chocolate Lab, tail wagging madly, appeared on the run from the back of the house.

Grace loved dogs. She'd always wanted one, but working the hours she worked, she knew it would be the height of selfishness to indulge herself, for she couldn't give a dog the kind of time and attention it deserved.

She knelt down to pet the Lab, who had stopped in front of her. "Hey," she said, "what's *your* name?"

"That's Velvet," Margaret said. "My niece named her. Said her coat felt like velvet."

Grace let the dog nuzzle her for a moment, then stood. By now she'd shed her coat, gloves and scarf, and Margaret had removed Emily's hat and sweater.

"You can hang your coat here," Margaret said, head inclining toward a coat closet. "Then let's go back to the family room, shall we?" She was still carrying Emily.

Velvet, obviously torn between staying with the new person and following her mistress, trailed slowly behind, turning to look at Grace as if to say, *Aren't you coming?*

Grace picked up the infant seat and followed Margaret to the back of the house where the family room adjoined the big eat-in kitchen. A large brick fireplace dominated one end of the room, and a cheery fire burned within. Grace couldn't help smiling to see a fat calico cat sitting on the hearth, just as she'd imagined. Unlike Velvet, the cat's only acknowledgment of their presence was opening its green eyes for a few seconds, then closing them again.

"That's Daisy," Margaret said, following Grace's gaze. "She's a bit snooty."

"Aren't all cats? My mother always said that was because they know they're superior beings." The cat opened her eyes again and stared at Grace. Grace grinned. "Heard me, did you?" She turned to Margaret. "Where shall I put Emily's seat?"

"How about on the coffee table?"

Grace looked at the shining walnut surface. "Are you sure? It might scratch it. Why don't we put a towel or something under it?"

"Oh, I don't care about scratches," Margaret said. "It's just a table." She could hardly seem to tear her eyes from Emily.

Grace shrugged and put down the infant seat, making sure it was locked into its upright position. She reached for Emily. "She likes sitting in her chair."

"Oh, can't I hold her awhile longer?" Margaret said.

Before Grace could answer, Bruce walked into the room.

"I told Pete to come back for you at four," he said. "Is that all right?"

"That's fine." Grace turned back to Margaret. Emily seemed fascinated with her—her slate-blue eyes gazing steadily at Margaret's face. Margaret was murmuring to the baby, and as Grace watched, Emily smiled.

"Oh, look at her dimples!" Margaret exclaimed. "Bruce, did you see them?"

"I did." That tender smile was back on his face.

Grace didn't like herself at that moment. What was wrong with her? Why did she feel so territorial and…jealous? Yes, that was it. She was jealous of Margaret. Jealous of the confident way she held Emily. Jealous of her perfect home and her perfect husband and their perfect dog and cat. Jealous of the fact that Margaret and Bruce could give Emily everything, and she, Grace, could give her nothing.

Grace swallowed.

Except love.

Fighting to keep her emotions under control, Grace said, "I need to check Emily's diaper, then I should feed her."

Margaret smiled. "Oh, let me." Without waiting for Grace's answer, she added, "Do you have something to lay under her? I'll just change her here, on the sofa."

Once again, Grace wanted to say no, that she would do both, but how could she? She was going to let Margaret and Bruce *adopt* Emily, wasn't she? So why would she refuse Margaret such a natural request?

But something seemed to be pressing on Grace's chest the whole time she watched Margaret change and then feed Emily, cooing to her and smiling that radiant, luminous smile.

Margaret would make a wonderful mother, Grace could see that. Emily would want for nothing. She would live in this lovely, gracious home; she would have the best of everything, and most of all, she would be adored by two very nice people.

So why did Grace feel so miserable?

Why did she want to snatch Emily out of Margaret's arms and go running out the door?

Having a sister is like having a best friend you can't get rid of. You know whatever you do, they'll still be there.
—*Amy Li*

CHAPTER 9

Grace couldn't sleep that night. Over and over, she replayed the afternoon with the Standishes. Again and again, she told herself she was being crazy, that Bruce and Margaret were absolutely perfect potential parents for Emily. Perfect.

With them, Emily would grow up secure, loved and have every opportunity for the kind of future most young women only dreamed about.

Margaret would be there to take her to dancing lessons, shopping, to museums on school holidays. She would be there when Emily went to school in the mornings and when she came home in the afternoons. She'd teach Emily to knit or crochet, to garden, to cook.

What could Grace do for Emily?

Letting the Standishes adopt Emily was the right thing to do. Yet every time she thought about packing up Emily's things and handing her over, her emotions took over, and her stomach felt hollow and her heart hurt and she felt as if she couldn't breathe.

Please, God, tell me what to do....

Grace tossed and turned, and every time she started to doze off, she would jerk awake, sweating, her heart pounding. She knew she was having a panic attack, and she tried to calm herself. Emily slept through her two o'clock feeding, not waking until three. Grace was grateful to have something to do. She got up, changed the baby's wet diaper, warmed a bottle of milk, then brought Emily into bed with her. After feeding and burping her, Emily fell asleep against Grace's shoulder. Grace gently put her down and curled up beside her, pulling the blanket and comforter over both of them.

For the rest of the night, Grace lay awake listening to the baby's breathing and the occasional squeaks and grunts she made in her sleep.

A few minutes before six, she turned off the alarm before it sounded and eased herself out of bed. Emily slept on, and Grace hated to move her. But even though the experts said most babies didn't have strong enough neck muscles to roll over on their own until they were at least four months old, it made Grace nervous to leave Emily untended in her bed. So she very carefully picked her up and carried her to the other bedroom and her crib. The baby stirred, scrunching herself up, but quickly settled back into sleep.

Grace stood over the crib for a long moment just watching her. *I love her,* she thought. *How can I give her away?*

But if she kept her, she still had all the problems she'd ever had. A job that demanded most of her time. And a child-care crisis she still hadn't solved.

Thursday would be Alexis's last day. Three days. Whether or not she ultimately gave Emily to the Standishes—for the adoption wouldn't happen immediately—Grace only had three days to find someone to care for Emily in the interim.

Leaving the door to the baby's room open, she quickly showered and dressed. By then the coffee—on a timer to start at six-thirty—was ready, and she poured herself a mugful. She checked Emily again, marveling that the baby was still soundly asleep. Carrying the coffee back to her bedroom, Grace sat at her desk and pulled out her checkbook and calculator.

When Alexis arrived at seven-thirty, Grace had formulated a plan. Her child-care problem was a result of her belief that she could have her cake and eat it, too. But she now realized the only way she could even think about keeping Emily was to make some compromises. The first order of business would be to find reliable live-in care for the baby, because her experience with Alexis had shown her the girl was right. With Grace's unpredictable hours, she absolutely had to have a live-in. Which meant that in the short term, Grace and Emily would have to share a room, so whoever Grace hired could have a room of her own.

Later, after Grace got her partnership, she could afford a bigger apartment, one with three bedrooms. But for now, she would buy herself a twin-size bed and move her own queen-size one into the spare room. Unfortunately, they would have to share the bathroom, but hopefully, that wouldn't present an insurmountable problem, not if Grace explained to a prospective employee that the situation was only temporary.

Alexis frowned when she saw Grace dressed in jeans and a red sweater. "Aren't you going to work?"

"Not today. I have some other things I have to take care of."

"Oh, okay. Um, Ms. Campisi, have you found someone else to watch Emily?"

"Not yet. Why? Has something changed? Can you stay on, after all?"

Alexis shook her head. "No, I just wondered, that's all. You haven't said anything."

"I've been trying to figure out what to do," Grace said.

"I really am sorry, Ms. Campisi."

"I know you are, Alexis. Don't worry about it. I understand your position."

"I just don't want you to be mad."

Grace studied Alexis's expression. She recognized sympathy, but there was something else. "Don't worry, Alexis. I'll give you a glowing recommendation. I know this has turned out differently than both of us had hoped." She sighed. "I'm not mad. I realize this is my problem to solve. Now," she said brightly, "I'm going to go into my bedroom and shut the door so I can make some phone calls and get some things done on the computer. Emily was still asleep when I last looked in on her."

"Thank you, Ms. Campisi. I'm sure you know how important it is to keep a good reputation when you're caring for children." Alexis smiled. "I'll go check on Emily now."

Grace waited until eight to call her office. She told Jamie she was taking a personal day, and after they'd gone over her calendar and she'd given Jamie instructions on rescheduling and reassigning, she called Amelia Burton, the woman she'd talked to at the nanny agency about live-in help.

Amelia said she was delighted to hear that Grace had worked out a way to provide a private room for live-in help and said she'd see what she could do about lining up some interviews for Grace.

"This afternoon," Grace said. "I'm in a bind. I have to hire someone just as soon as possible."

"I'll call you back within the hour," Amelia promised. "I have two women in mind. Both are eager to get back to work."

Grace logged onto her e-mail account at the office and took care of answering the most urgent messages while she waited for the call back. She could hear Alexis talking to Emily from the next room. It was interesting to note how little Emily cried now compared to how much she'd cried when Perry had been taking care of her. The experts said that babies picked up on the emotional undercurrents in a household, that if the mother or caregiver was stressed and unhappy, the baby was likely to sleep less and cry more. The change in Emily coincided with Perry's leaving, a fact that couldn't be a coincidence.

Forty minutes after they'd hung up, Amelia Burton called back. "Both of the women I mentioned earlier said they'd love to talk to you about the job."

"Great," Grace said.

"Have you got a fax machine?" Amelia asked.

"Not here at the apartment."

"What about e-mail?"

"Yes, I've got that."

"Then I'll send the two résumés via e-mail attachment. That way you'll have a chance to study them before the two candidates arrive."

When they hung up, Grace felt more hopeful than she had since Perry had left. Maybe this time, things really would work out.

Because the first interview wasn't until two o'clock, Grace used the intervening time to make a fast trip to Straight from the Crate, where she bought a twin-size bed, a comfortable chair and matching ottoman, a small bookcase, a dresser and mirror, a nightstand and a good reading lamp. Luckily, she was able to make arrangements to have the furniture delivered on Wednesday, so the room would be ready for a new nanny.

She crossed her fingers and prayed that one of the women she interviewed today would work out.

* * *

The next morning, as soon as Grace got to the office, she called Bruce Standish. When she said she needed to talk to him, he said he was free for the next hour.

"I'm so sorry, Bruce," she said after they were settled with the door closed. "I spent a sleepless night on Sunday after leaving your place, and I have finally realized I just can't give Emily up."

He looked stricken, the color draining from his face. For a long moment, he just looked at her. "Margaret will be devastated," he finally said. "She's already started making all kinds of plans."

"I know," Grace said miserably. "I feel terrible about getting your hopes up. I really thought giving Emily up for adoption was the best thing for her and for me, but I—I just can't do it. It's going to be tough, but I want to keep her."

She could see how he was struggling to keep his emotions in check, and she felt so bad for him. "I'm sorry," she said again, knowing it was inadequate.

He nodded. "Me, too."

For a long moment, they sat in silence. Grace felt like a worm. And even though she didn't want to, she couldn't help wondering if she had irreparably hurt her candidacy for the partnership. Would her change of heart concerning Emily cause Bruce to talk against her when the partners voted? Surely not. Surely he wasn't like that. But the thought frightened her. She *had* to get that partnership. How else would she carry through with her plans?

"How are you going to manage?" he finally asked.

"What do you mean?"

"Come on, Grace, you know what I mean. You're a single woman, and you work sixty hours a week. We all do."

"I've hired someone who's going to live in." In fact, Rose Mooney, the woman she'd hired, was starting tomorrow so that Alexis could show her the ropes.

He nodded, seemed to hesitate, then said, "Do you still want that partnership?"

Her heart jumped, but she kept her voice steady. "Of course, I do. Why would you think I wouldn't?"

He heaved a sigh. "Frankly, even with live-in help, I don't see how you can do the job *and* raise Emily. Her presence has already impacted your performance here."

Grace stiffened. "That's not true. Tell me one thing I've neglected to do. Why, I work my butt off for this firm, and you know it." Oh, shit. Why couldn't she have said that in a more diplomatic way?

But Bruce didn't seem to take offense. He just returned her gaze levelly. "Look, I like you. And before Emily became a part of your life, I would have agreed with you wholeheartedly. But you should know that Neil Braddock has complained about you. He sent an e-mail to the other senior partners saying he didn't think you could be counted on to do the job we need done."

Grace gritted her teeth. Damn Neil Braddock. He was such a prick. Once. Once she'd said no to him.

"You know how he is, Grace," Bruce said softly.

"Yes, I know."

"You need to be careful, very careful, from now on."

"When will the vote take place?"

"We're meeting Friday afternoon."

"*This* Friday?"

"Yes."

"Tell me something, Bruce. Will you vote for me? Or do you feel the way Neil does?"

"I still think you're the best candidate for the job."

"What about Wallace?"

"Grace, you know I can't discuss this with you. I've already said more than I should have. I do know that he's been pleased with your work in the past."

Grace's heart sank. "And now?"

"I don't know."

Grace's mind was spinning when she left Bruce's office. Would they do that? Would she be punished for trying to do a good thing? But even as she thought about it, she knew they could and probably would.

What am I going to do?

The sad thing, and the thing Grace hated to admit to herself, was that if she were one of the senior partners, she would probably vote against her, too.

It is true that I was born in Iowa, but I can't speak for my twin sister.

—*Abigail Van Buren*

CHAPTER 10

When Grace got home at seven-thirty, there was a message from Doug on her voice mail. He'd already left one with Jamie at the office and another on her cell phone. All three messages said he was back from London where he'd been a featured speaker at an international symposium and that he'd missed her and was eager to talk to her.

She sighed wearily. She guessed she'd have to call him. She'd been putting it off because she simply hadn't had the energy to deal with anything more.

"You look tired," Alexis said.

Grace nodded. "I am." Wrenching her mind from the conversation with Bruce and the upcoming call to Doug, she said more brightly, "How's Emily been today?"

Alexis frowned. "She's been a bit fussy. I have the feeling she might not be feeling a hundred percent."

Grace felt a twinge of alarm. "I hope she's not getting sick."

"She's not feverish or anything like that," Alexis said. "Just not as sunny as usual. But don't worry," she added, "I'm sure she'll be fine tomorrow. We all have off days, even babies."

Grace hoped Alexis was right. She probably was. After all, she knew a lot more about babies than Grace did. *Please, please don't let Emily get sick....*

"I've already given her a bath and she's had her seven o'clock feeding."

"Is she asleep?"

Alexis nodded. "I just checked on her five minutes ago."

Grace thought longingly about a nap herself, but there was too much to do in preparation for Rose Mooney's arrival tomorrow, not to mention that dreaded phone call to Doug.

After Alexis left, Grace went into her bedroom where the baby's crib was now installed next to Grace's desk. The only light came from the night-light and the open door. Grace looked at Emily for a long moment, drinking in her sweetness and innocence, which soothed her, then reluctantly turned away.

She undressed inside her closet, grateful it had a light and was large enough to do so, because she had the feeling she'd be doing a lot of it in the near future. She put on her sweats and thick socks, then headed for the kitchen. She poured herself a glass of wine, then picked up her cell phone and called Doug.

"I was beginning to think you were avoiding me," he said.

"No, I've just been in the middle of a crisis, that's all."

"Work? Or personal?"

"Both." She took a deep breath. "Perry's gone, Doug. She walked out, leaving the baby at my office."

"What? When did this happen?"

"It's almost a month now."

"Almost a month," he repeated.

"Yes."

"I was in New York then."

"I know."

"Why didn't you call me?"

"Because I was upset enough, Doug. I didn't need another lecture."

He was silent for a long moment. "So what's happening now?" he finally said.

"I've decided to keep Emily. I'm going to petition to legally adopt her." Grace was stunned to realize that was *exactly* what she planned to do, no matter what happened with the partnership.

"I see," he said. His voice was noticeably cooler. "You know, Grace, I was offered a fantastic job in London, and I was actually thinking about turning it down because of you. But maybe I'll take it now, because you obviously didn't consider me at all when you made this decision."

"It's not like we're married, Doug. Didn't we decide from the very beginning that our relationship would always be no-strings?"

"So this is it, then? We're saying goodbye, nice to know you."

"I think that would be best, don't you?" she said softly. "It was fun while it lasted, but now we both have different priorities."

"What about your job? How the hell are you going to manage a partnership—that's if you still get it—and raising a child?"

Grace sighed. "I'm awfully tired, Doug. I don't feel like getting into a long discussion about how difficult my future is going to be. Talking about it serves no purpose, and it's not going to change my mind."

This time the silence between them was filled with tension. *Just hang up*, Grace thought. *Get mad and hang up*.

"Fine," he said. "It's been nice knowing you, Grace. Good luck. You're certainly going to need it."

And with that, he broke the connection.

Funny, Grace thought later as she fixed herself a bowl of tomato soup and some crackers and cheese to go with it, but she didn't feel sad at all. In fact, all she felt was relief.

Grace didn't get into the office until ten o'clock Thursday morning because she'd wanted to be at home for the first hour or so after Rose Mooney had arrived. Rose was in her fifties, a widow with two grown children—a son in the air force and a married daughter in Philadelphia—and she had a charming trace of an Irish brogue, even though, as she had told Grace earlier, she'd lived in New York for more than thirty years.

"Oh, what a darlin' baby," she'd crooned when she'd seen Emily. "Hello there, precious."

After an hour with both Rose and Alexis, Grace had known she could leave for work with confidence.

"Mr. Finn wants to see you," Jamie said when Grace walked into her office.

"Does he know I was at home?"

"He didn't ask. Just said to tell you to call him when you got in."

"Thanks, Jamie."

When Grace called, Wallace said, "Come to my office, Grace. I'd rather we talked face-to-face."

Grace fought the ominous feeling in her stomach as she walked to Wallace Finn's large corner office, the nicest one at the firm.

"Have a seat, Grace," Wallace said when his secretary showed her into his office. He was standing behind his desk.

"Can I get you some coffee?" the secretary asked.

"No, thanks, Donna. I'm fine." Grace was jumpy enough without added caffeine. She tried to read Wallace Finn's expression as he sat down again. She wondered if he knew she'd decided to keep Emily.

"How are things going with you?" he asked. "Lucille said she'd given you some help with finding child care."

"Yes, she was very helpful." She shrugged. "It's been a little rough." She decided it was best to be as honest as possible. "But I think everything's going to work out okay now."

"I talked to Bruce last night."

"Oh." So he did know.

"I respect you for wanting to raise your sister's baby, Grace, but I can't help thinking you've bitten off a lot."

"Yes, I know I have, but I just hired a live-in nanny, so things should be much easier from now on."

He nodded, regarding her steadily. Then he sighed and said, "Grace, I feel it's only fair to tell you that I am going to recommend the new partnership be offered to Jack Townsend."

Grace's heart knocked painfully, and she could feel the blood rushing to her head. She gripped the arms of her chair to keep them from trembling. Her voice was unsteady when she said, "But, Wallace...why?"

"Come on, Grace, you know why. In the past couple of months you've taken personal leave, you've been late, you've canceled appointments, you haven't been able to make meetings and much of the time when you've actually been in the office, you've been distracted. Your work has suffered because you've been worried about the baby. And that's only right. If you're going to raise her, she *should* be your first priority. I have no problem with that. But I can't, in good conscience, recommend you for this partnership. It's not fair to you and it's not fair to the firm."

Grace fought to control the anger and disappointment flooding her. When she replied, her voice was even. "What about all the years I've killed myself for this firm? Do they mean *nothing*?"

"Of course not, Grace. They mean a lot, to me in particular. You know how I feel about you. I hired you and I've considered myself your mentor, and I know you feel the same way. I respect you highly. But I'm practical, and I know you are, too. Right now you're emotional because you're disappointed. When you've had a chance to think about this, I believe you'll agree with me that taking on more responsibility and even longer hours than you're currently working is not in your best interest. It's certainly not in the baby's."

Grace looked away. Her gaze landed on the silver-framed picture he kept at the right-hand corner of his desk. It was a family photo of him, Lucille, their children and grandchildren. It had been taken a year earlier, at Christmas. The huge fir tree in the background provided a festive setting. One of his grandchildren—a little girl—was sitting on her mother's knee. The mother was his daughter Melanie, an accountant who had quit her job a month before the baby had been born.

In that moment, Grace knew there was nothing more to say. Wearily, she stood. "Thank you, Wallace, for being honest with me." She turned to leave.

"Wait, Grace, don't go. I have a proposition for you."

Wanting nothing but to escape to lick her wounds, Grace turned back reluctantly.

"Despite what you may think now," Wallace said gently, "we value you here, Grace."

She swallowed, not trusting herself to speak.

"We don't want you to leave."

Funny. Grace hadn't even considered leaving. "Thank you, Wallace. I appreciate that." But maybe now she would.

"I want you to think about something."

"All right."

"How would you like to work part-time?"

Grace blinked. "Part-time?"

"Yes. You'd be assigned to however many cases you felt you wanted to undertake. As long as you gave us, say, thirty hours a week, we'd be happy. If you wanted or needed to work more hours to get the job done, that would be fine, too."

"How would I be paid?"

"By the hour." He named a figure.

Grace did some quick calculations. Even if she worked a forty-hour week, she wouldn't bring in enough to keep a live-in nanny. "What about benefits? Bonuses?"

"You'd still keep your benefits but you'd no longer be eligible for bonuses. You would, however, share in any large judgments won on any of your assigned cases."

Grace met his gaze. "How much time do I have to decide?"

"There's no timetable. Just think about it and let me know. If you prefer to keep working a full schedule, that's fine, too." His expression softened. "I know the loss of the partnership is a blow, Grace. And I really am sorry."

"Thank you, Wallace. I am, too."

If Grace hadn't had the baby to think about, she would have gone home and drunk a whole bottle of wine that night. But she *did* have Emily, so drowning her sorrows wasn't an option.

Instead, she comforted herself by ordering a big double-cheese and mushroom pizza, which she ate after she got Emily down for the night. This would be her last night alone in the apartment, for Rose was moving in tomorrow. The furniture Grace had purchased had been delivered that afternoon and, between Alexis and Rose, they'd fixed up Rose's bedroom and moved all of Emily's things into Grace's room.

Grace had also made arrangements with the super to store her exercise equipment and a few other pieces she no longer had room for. It was costing her extra, but someday she hoped to have room for everything again.

It was hard to give up her dream of a partnership in the firm. She'd been so single-minded in her goal that she now felt like a train that had suddenly been derailed. But the partnership was gone, so instead of continuing to bemoan its loss, she'd better turn her energies to figuring out where she was going to go from here.

She fell asleep thinking about Wallace's suggestion of part-time work and by the time she got to the office the next morning, she'd already made a mental list of people she needed to call before making a decision. But first she needed to tell Jamie about the partnership.

"Oh, no!" Jamie said.

"I'm sorry, Jamie," Grace said. They were sitting in Grace's office with the door closed. "I know you were counting on it."

"Well, yes, I was, and it's hard to give up the promise of more money and everything, but it's *you* I feel the worst for. You've worked so hard, Grace. This just stinks!"

Grace was warmed by Jamie's loyalty. "I can't really blame Wallace. He's right, you know. Having Emily has changed everything, and I probably *couldn't* do the job they'd want from me." She sighed heavily. "The truth is, in some ways, this decision is a relief." Her smile was wry. "Now I don't have to try to be superwoman."

"Oh, Grace." Jamie got up, came around to the back of Grace's desk and leaned down to hug her. "I'm really, really sorry about this, but I admire you for what you're doing."

Grace was so touched, she didn't know what to say. She'd always known Jamie liked her, but they'd never been touchy-feely. It wasn't Grace's style. She'd always believed co-workers should keep a friendly but business-like approach to their relationship. "Thank you. I appreciate that more than you know."

When Jamie left Grace's office to go back to her own, Grace opened her business-card folder and searched until she found the one she wanted. Jeff Hunter. He'd worked part-time for the firm several years earlier. She hoped his number hadn't changed.

She was lucky. It hadn't. "Jeff," she said when he answered. "This is Grace Campisi from Finn, Braddock and Morgan."

"Hey. How are you, Grace?"

"I'm fine. Just fine. And you?"

"Doing great. Ann and I have a new baby boy. We just brought him home from the hospital yesterday."

Grace smiled at the pride in his voice. "Congratulations. Listen, Jeff, the reason I called is that I wanted to talk to you about doing part-time work."

"Uh, I no longer do part-time work, Grace. I work for Marshall and Fitch. The only reason you found me at home today is because I've taken some time off to help Ann."

"I'm sorry, I didn't make myself clear. I'm thinking of going to part-time here at Finn, Braddock and Morgan, and I had some questions about your experience with it."

"Oh, okay, shoot. I'll be happy to tell you whatever I can."

"My first question is, were you able to keep regular hours? For instance, if I didn't want to work past five o'clock on any given day, is that reasonable?"

He laughed. "You're not serious, are you?"

"So that's not reasonable?"

"Not at *your* firm. Hell, Grace, some nights I was there till ten or later. Just depended on the case. On the other hand, some days I didn't have to work at all. But I never knew in advance."

They talked awhile longer, but Jeff had answered the most important question. Even doing part-time work, Grace would probably need a live-in. And since that wouldn't be possible with the reduction in income she could expect, part-time work wasn't going to be an option.

Which left her exactly where?

An older sister helps one remain half child, half woman.

—*Author Unknown*

CHAPTER 11

Grace had just gotten Emily down for the night when the phone rang. Caller ID showed an unfamiliar number. She almost didn't answer, but then she realized it could be Perry and hurriedly pressed the Talk button before the call revolved to voice mail.

"Hello?"

"Grace?"

"Perry! It *is* you. Thank God. Where *are* you? Why haven't you called? Mom's worried sick."

"Please don't be angry, Grace. I—I'm in Vegas, but we probably won't be staying here." Her voice broke. "Don had an accident."

"What kind of accident?"

"He…was riding a friend's motorcycle and he rear-ended a car."

Grace closed her eyes.

"It wasn't his fault, Grace. The woman stopped dead in front of him. He couldn't help hitting her."

"Just tell me one thing, Perry. Are you coming back? Have you changed your mind about Emily?"

Perry didn't immediately answer.

Grace held her breath. Although she would never have believed this a few months ago, she didn't want Perry to come back and claim Emily again.

"I'm sorry, Grace, but I'm not coming back. We…we're going back to San Diego. Don has a brother there. He said we can stay with him until Don's out of his cast and can work again."

"Okay, fine. But there are some things you need to do for me."

"What?"

"You can't just say you want me to raise Emily. That just doesn't work for me, because if I'm going to do this, I want it to be legal. There are forms you're going to have to sign and maybe other things the court will require. That means I'm going to need a phone number where I can contact you."

"I—I'll sign whatever you need, but I don't have a phone number to give you. All Don's brother has is a cell phone, and I don't know the number."

Grace rolled her eyes. Of course Perry wouldn't have a number. Normal people got phone numbers and addresses. But Perry never did anything the way normal people did. "For crying out loud, Perry, can't you just ask Don for it?"

"I…no. I—I can't do that. Not…not now. He's too upset over the accident and everything."

"Can I ask you something?" Without waiting for Perry to answer, Grace said, "What the *hell* are you doing with a man you're afraid to ask a simple question? A *reasonable* question."

"I-I'll get the number, but I can't do it right now."

Grace sighed.

"Grace?" Perry said in a small voice. "I-is Emily okay?"

"Do you really *care?*" The moment the words were out of Grace's mouth, she wished she could take them back.

"H-how can you say that, Grace? You know I love her. That's why I left. Because I wanted her to have a good life." Perry started to cry.

"Oh, God, Perry, I'm sorry. I don't know why I'm such a bitch sometimes. Please don't cry. Emily's fine. You should see her. She's so beautiful. She's growing like a weed."

"Is she?" Perry sounded pathetic.

"Yes. And I think she looks like you." This was an exaggeration because Grace had a feeling the baby looked exactly like her unknown father with her heart-shaped face, her deep dimples—none of the Campisis had dimples—and her slate-blue eyes.

"She does?"

"She definitely has your hair. It's just as curly and just as dark. Her eyes are different, though. They're a gorgeous grayish-blue."

"Like her dad's," Perry said softly. "That's what I liked about him. His eyes. He…he was cute." She took an audible breath. "You're not mad at me, are you, Grace? I didn't know what else to do when I left Emily with you."

"No, I'm not mad at you. In fact, when I said I wanted all this to be legal...I meant I want to adopt Emily." She smiled when she said it, for suddenly she knew it was exactly what she wanted to do.

"You *do*?"

"I do. Will you give your consent?"

"Will...can I see her sometimes?"

"Of course you can. I want her to know you. You're her mother."

"No, Grace," Perry said sadly, "you're going to be her mother. I'll be happy just to be her aunt and see her once in a while."

Suddenly Grace felt like crying herself. "I remember the day you were born as if it were yesterday."

"Really?"

"I was so excited. I was in chemistry class and Mr. McDougal said there was a phone call for me. I knew it was Dad. When he told me I had a baby sister, I was thrilled. I went around bragging to everyone."

"Are you still thrilled to have me for a sister?" Perry said after a long moment.

"I love you, Perry. That'll never change."

"I love you, too, Grace." After a moment, she added in a brisker tone, "What do you need me to do so you can adopt Emily?"

"I'll need a notarized document saying you are voluntarily giving up your parental rights and that you agree with my desire to adopt your child. I can draw up the document and overnight it to you and then, once you sign it, you can take it somewhere and get it notarized and have it sent back to me."

"But I don't have an address yet. For you to send me something in San Diego, I mean."

"Can't you stay where you are just one more day? I can get the document to you no later than tomorrow afternoon."

"I—I can't, Grace. Don wants to leave in the morning."

"How are you getting to San Diego, anyway?"

"I'm driving us," Perry said, so low Grace almost didn't hear her.

"Then you have control over when you leave. Tell him you have to wait for something important."

"Grace, I—I can't." She sounded miserable. "He'll be mad. He's in a really bad mood right now."

I do love her, but I'd still like to smack her silly. "That's too bad, isn't it? He's dependent on you since he can't drive and you can. So he'll have to do whatever you say."

"Grace, you just don't know…he…he'll be furious."

"Tough. He ought to be kissing the ground you walk on, because I'm assuming you're going to be taking care of him once you get to this brother's house, right?"

"Yes, but—"

"No buts. For once in your life, just take charge and do it. I mean, what's he gonna do? He might sulk for a couple of days, but he'll get over it."

"I can't, Grace. I just can't. You don't know him. He'll be so mad, and he'll make my life miserable for days. It's…it's just not worth it. I'll call you the minute we get to his brother's and give you an address. I promise."

Grace wanted to scream, but she managed to say, "And when will that be?" calmly enough.

"We'll be there tomorrow night. I'll call you on Sunday."

"You'll have to call me at Sal's then. I'm planning to go out there for the weekend."

"Oh. Okay. Does… Do he and Michael know you have Emily?"

"Of course they know. So does Mom. What they don't know is that I'm going to keep her. They think I'm giving her to a lawyer at my firm to adopt."

"Grace! You wouldn't do that! I don't want someone else having Emily. I want you to have her."

"And what if I hadn't been able to keep her? Then what?"

"But you can. You said you want to."

Grace heaved another sigh. Why argue? Emily's future was settled. Grace wanted her. And Perry was agreeable. Why fight? "Do you have Sal's number?"

"Yeah. It's in my wallet."

"And you'll call me Sunday?"

"Yes, I promise."

"Because I'm telling you, Perry, no matter how much I love you, if I don't hear from you on Sunday, first thing Monday morning I'm going to family court and I'm going to petition the court to terminate your parental rights on the grounds of abandonment."

Silence.

"I mean it, Perry."

"I know you mean it. I—I'll call you, Grace. Sunday."

"Good. And please be careful driving to San Diego. I don't want anything to happen to you."

"I will be. I—I love you, Grace."

Grace nodded wearily. "I know. I love you, too."

Perry fought to keep her emotions under control after her conversation with Grace. For one thing, what good did crying do? What was done was done, and no amount of waterworks would change it. For another, she didn't want Don to know how she felt. He thought she was perfectly happy without Emily, and he'd be upset if he knew how much she thought about the baby.

Why couldn't he be different? Why couldn't he love kids? Because even this short stay with Bud and Peggy had been enough to show Perry that his objection to raising Emily had less to do with her being someone else's kid than it had to do with the fact that he really didn't like kids. Even though Perry wasn't all that crazy about Bud, he and Peggy had two cute little boys, three and five. And it was obvious to Perry, at least, that Don barely tolerated them, even when they were on their best behavior.

But maybe he'd be different with his own kid.

Surely he would.

"Perry! Where the hell are you?"

Perry jumped up. She'd taken the phone into the bathroom so Don wouldn't hear her calling Grace. Opening the bathroom door, she called, "I'm coming. I was in the bathroom." She flushed the toilet, waited a minute, then walked through the kitchen, where she put the phone back into its base before joining Don in the living room where he sat on a chair with his casted right leg resting on the matching ottoman. "What do you need?" she said.

Don's normally handsome face was scowling. His thick blond hair, his biggest vanity, had tufts standing up because he hadn't been able to wash it since the accident two days ago. "I want another beer, dammit."

"I'm sorry, honey. I'll go get it for you."

"Where *were* you, anyway?"

"I told you. In the bathroom. Um, are you hungry? Do you want something to eat?" It was nearly seven. Bud and Peggy and the kids had gone to her folks' house for dinner; Perry and Don were on their own.

"Let's order a pizza."

They'd already had pizza twice in the past three days, but Perry knew better than to argue. Not now while Don was in such a horrible mood. Of course, she understood why. He was hurting from all his scrapes and bruises, his sore back and his broken leg, and he was frustrated because he knew he wouldn't be able to work for weeks, maybe months. If the accident had happened on a job, he'd be covered by workmen's comp and he'd have sick pay or something. Now, though, he'd get nothing. In fact, the insurance company of the woman he'd hit was saying the accident was Don's fault, so who knew what would happen?

"Okay, I'll order a pizza," she said. She walked over to him. "Want me to fix that pillow behind your back?"

He waved her off. "Christ, Perry, quit treating me like a baby or something. Just get me the damned beer!"

In the kitchen, Perry blotted her eyes. She knew Don didn't mean to hurt her feelings. He was just miserable right now. Telling herself things would be better when they got back in San Diego, she took a Bud out of the fridge, put a determined smile on her face, and walked back to the living room.

"Sal?"

"Oh, hey, Grace. How're things going with the adoption?"

"I'd like to talk to you about that. What are you and Jen doing today?" Sal still thought Grace was giving Emily to the Standishes.

"We were just talking about going to the garden center and buying some bedding plants, but we don't have to do that today. Why? What'd you have in mind?"

"I thought I'd bring Emily and come out for the weekend."

"The *weekend?* You're not *working* this weekend?"

Grace heard the incredulity. She smiled ruefully. Sal had never known her to take an entire weekend off. "Nope. Um, that's part of what I wanted to discuss with you. I need your advice."

He chuckled. "This is a red-letter day. I should write that down. What's the date? March 29th? Thirtieth? Grace is coming out. She wants my advice."

Grace couldn't help laughing. "Okay, smarty. That's enough."

"When're you coming?"

"We'll be on the eleven-ten train."

"I'll pick you up at the station."

Sal and Jen lived in Massapequa in a thirty-seven-year-old Cape Cod with four bedrooms. It was a cozy, comfortable home they'd purchased when their children were little, and even now, with only Julie at home—Drew was a sophomore in college—they saw no reason to move into something newer or more efficient.

Grace liked their house, but she would never have wanted the commute. That wasn't an issue with Sal and Jennifer. He worked out of the house—one of the bedrooms had been made into an office for him—and Jen was an insurance adjuster who worked the Long Island area almost exclusively and only had to make a trip to the Manhattan headquarters of her company for monthly meetings.

Grace indulged in a taxi to get her to the train station, and once she and Emily were settled in their seats, she enjoyed the ride out to the island.

A matronly woman with a friendly smile sat across from them. After a while, she said, "Your baby's beautiful."

Grace beamed. "Thank you." She loved it when people thought Emily was hers.

"How old is she?"

"She'll be eleven weeks old Monday."

"Well, she's just lovely. You're lucky."

"Yes," Grace agreed. "I'm *very* lucky."

For the remainder of the ride to the island, Grace basked in the admiring glances the woman continued to send her way. Who would have dreamed that she would feel so happy right now? She'd lost the partnership she'd worked for so long and so hard. She had no idea how she was going to manage both working and raising Emily. In fact, her entire life was upside down.

And yet, she *was* happy.

And she planned to be even happier.

Just as soon as she figured out what she was going to do and how she was going to do it.

As promised, Sal was waiting when the train pulled in. You couldn't miss his lanky six-foot-two frame, dark curly hair or bespectacled dark eyes. Although the sun was shining on this late March day, it was still cold, and Sal wore a red parka. Grace, too, was dressed warmly and she'd bundled Emily in a fleece one-piece outfit with enclosed feet, over which she'd put a yellow jacket with a hood. And for good measure, she'd wrapped a yellow-and-green quilt around the baby.

Sal hurried over to help Grace off the train, enveloped her in a quick hug, then reached for her bags, which the attendant handed down.

Only after that did he look at Emily. His expression softened into tenderness. "She's beautiful," he said, his voice gruff with emotion. "Look at that black hair."

"A true Campisi," Grace said.

He nodded, his eyes suspiciously shiny. Sal was a softy. Tough on the outside, a marshmallow inside. He loved kids, dogs, old people; he even loved teenagers. Grace had known he'd be immediately taken with his new little niece, and she hadn't been wrong.

Emily regarded her uncle with unblinking eyes.

"She's taking your measure."

"Hope I don't come up short."

"My big brother? Never."

At forty-six, Sal was four years older than Grace. As a kid he'd always tried to protect her, and she'd been fierce about pushing him away, saying she could take care of herself. But she'd loved him for wanting to. She still did. Sal was one of the good guys.

He was also one of the most levelheaded, intelligent men she'd ever known. He could take a problem, analyze it, see all sides, and almost always come up with a sensible suggestion.

This ability had served him well in his profession as a CPA. Now Grace hoped it would serve her well. Because if anyone needed a solution to what seemed like an impossible problem, she did.

Write your sister's weak points in the sand and her strong points in stone.

—*Author Unknown*

CHAPTER 12

"Here's how I see your problem, Grace."

Grace squeezed lemon into her tea. She, Jen and Sal had just finished lunch and were sitting and talking at the kitchen table. Emily lay contentedly in her carrier and watched them while Sal's and Jen's West Highland terrier, Gus, watched her. He'd been fascinated by the baby from the moment he'd set eyes on her. Grace almost got up to get her new digital camera out of her overnight bag, because she knew the dog and baby would make an adorable picture. Reluctantly, she tore her gaze away and turned her attention back to Sal. "I know what the problem is, Sal. What I need is a solution."

Sal grinned. "The solution is as plain as the nose on your face."

"I'm all ears."

"Your trouble is, you're stuck in a rut with your

thinking. What you should be doing is thinking outside the box."

"I don't know what you mean. What box?"

"The box that says you have to stay at the firm."

"I've thought of going somewhere else, but all law firms are the same, Sal. If I'm going to make enough money to support myself and Emily, I'll be at a firm where I'm expected to put in seventy-hour weeks. So why change? At least at Finn, Braddock and Morgan, they know me and my abilities, and my clients love me. And the truth is, I love the work, even if I don't have a partnership." This last was said with a grimace.

"Why do you have to stay in Manhattan? In fact, why stay in New York at all?"

Grace stared at her brother. Not stay in New York? The idea had never occurred to her.

"With your experience and credentials, you can go anywhere you want to go, Grace. If it were me, I'd do some research, find somewhere that's cheap to live and has a slower pace of life."

Move somewhere else. Grace thought about how many times she'd wished for a warmer climate.

"I can see the wheels turning," Sal said softly.

Jen smiled. "Me, too."

"If I'm going to go somewhere else, the logical thing would be for me to move to Florida," Grace said.

Sal raised his eyebrows. "Now that's a thought."

Jen looked at Grace. "Would you want to be that close to your mother?"

"I wouldn't have to go to Seacrest."

"If you moved to Florida and picked someplace other than Seacrest, your mother would have a fit," Jen said.

Grace nodded. Not Florida then. And yet, wouldn't moving to Seacrest be the perfect solution? Although Grace might not make much profit on the sale of her apartment, she'd recoup her down payment, which had been substantial. With that and her savings, she'd have enough to last her quite a while in Seacrest, maybe even a year if she was careful. "It might not be so bad to be in the same town as Mom. I mean, Aunt Mutt's there, too."

Sal smiled. "Why don't you call her? Sound her out about it? See what she thinks?"

"I will." Her mind spun with the possibilities Sal's suggestion had opened. "You know, in a small town like Seacrest, I could open up my own law office," she said wonderingly. "I could be like Isabelle Frank."

Sal gave her a quizzical smile. "Who's Isabelle Frank?"

"She's this really brilliant former A.D.A. who opened a storefront law office in Brooklyn. They did a feature on her in the *Times* one Sunday a year or so ago. She brought both her baby and her German shepherd to the office with her. Had a playpen and a crib and a sitter. All in one big room. Her clients loved it." Grace grinned. "Most of her clients were women. With women's issues."

"There you go," Sal said. "Now you're thinking outside the box."

Grace jumped up, went around the table, put her arms around Sal and kissed his cheek. "I knew you'd help me."

"Let's celebrate," said Jen. "I've got a bottle of spumante in the fridge. Let's open it."

Sal looked at the clock. "It's only two o'clock."

"What's your point?" Jen said.

"Yeah," Grace echoed. "Just what *is* your point?"

"Never mind," Sal said, laughing. "I know when I'm outnumbered."

The remainder of the weekend seemed to fly by. Saturday night they sat around the fire in the living room and played a lively game of Monopoly, followed by some cutthroat Scrabble. About ten o'clock, Julie, their sixteen-year-old daughter, came home from an all-day church-group outing, and Gus went nuts, barking and running around joyfully in between licking Julie's face dozens of times.

Julie, who looked like her mother with the same dark blond hair and blue eyes, laughed and hugged the wriggling dog. Watching them, Grace thought, *Why, I might even be able to have a dog if I leave the city!*

Her next thought was *And someday Emily will be a lovely teenager like her cousin and I'll be beaming proudly just like Sal and Jen are doing now....*

Her gaze moved to Emily, who lay on a quilt in front of the fire. Grace's heart clutched with a painful mixture of love and fear. God, she was so innocent. Her entire future depended on Grace and the decisions she made.

Please, God, don't let me fail her....

On Sunday morning the family always went to nine-thirty Mass at nearby St. Rose of Lima. When Sal gave Grace a questioning look, she said, "What about Emily?"

"What about her?" he countered.

"Just take along a pacifier or a bottle," Jen said. "I always took the kids to church when they were babies."

So Grace, who hadn't been to Mass in years, went to church with her family. And a funny thing happened while she was there. The stress of the past weeks receded, and a serenity she hadn't felt in a long time settled like a comforting cloak over her shoulders. The responses came naturally—like riding a bicycle, once learned, they were never forgotten.

Sal glanced over and smiled at her several times, and Grace thought about how dear her siblings were to her. During Communion, she even sang the hymn, an old familiar one called "Taste and See."

Afterward, walking out with Sal, Jen and Julie, she realized that losing that partnership didn't seem very important at all anymore.

I have Emily and a new life to look forward to, one that can be a lot better than my old life.

And suddenly, she could hardly wait to get started.

It wasn't until Grace and Emily were on the train heading back to Manhattan that Grace realized Perry had never called. *Maybe there's a message for me at home*. Grace whipped out her cell phone, intending to call her voice mail and check, but there was no service on the train. She'd have to wait until she got to the apartment.

But when she and a sleeping Emily arrived, Grace took one look at the phone and knew there was no message because the red light wasn't blinking.

Fine, Grace thought. She'd given Perry a chance, and Perry had once again blown it. So tomorrow, first thing, Grace would go over to family court and file her petition.

No, not first.

Second.

First she'd give Wallace her two-weeks notice.

Jamie's mouth dropped open. "You're *quitting?*" she squeaked.

"Yes, and I wanted you to be the first to know. In fact, I'd like you to type up a letter of resignation so that I can give it to Wallace after I tell him," Grace said. It was Monday morning. Grace had just arrived at work.

Thirty minutes later, letter in hand, Grace walked down to Wallace's office.

"Is there anything I can do to change your mind?" he asked after she'd told him.

Grace shook her head. "No. This is the right thing for me to do, Wallace." She smiled ruefully. "It's not the way I thought my life would turn out, but now that it has, I'm actually pretty happy about it."

He nodded. "Well, if that's the case, then I'm happy for you. I just hate to lose you. You're one of our brightest stars. If not for recent circumstances…"

"I know."

"Couldn't you at least stay until the Eagleton Energy case is settled? You know the judgment's going to be huge. And you'll be entitled to a nice share of it."

Grace sighed. "I know, but that case might go on for years before the firm sees a dime. You know that. And now that I've decided what I want to do, I want to get on with it. Besides, I don't want to miss out on any more of Emily's first year than I have to." She smiled at him. "But I'll stay as long as I can. Before I can move, I have to sell my apartment, anyway."

"The way apartments are selling in this city, it might sell the first day you put it on the market," he said.

"You'll still have me here for two weeks."

"Where are you planning to go?"

"I'm not positive, but I think I'm going to move to Florida. I talked to my mother and my aunt last night, and they're both thrilled by the idea."

He smiled with approval. They talked awhile more, then she stood, saying, "Well, I'd better get back and get started on my day. I've got work stacked up to the ceiling."

He stood, too, and walked around the desk. Putting his arm around her shoulder, he gave her a fatherly squeeze. "I'm going to miss you, Grace."

Grace swallowed against a sudden lump in her throat. "I'll miss you, too."

And yet, as she walked back to her office, she knew that she wouldn't miss much else. Jamie. She'd miss Jamie. And she'd miss the money.

But other than that…who cared?

She felt like skipping and shouting, both of which were very un-Grace-like things to do. But it was exciting thinking about all the upcoming changes in her life. Changes that promised to be not just challenging, but fun. Okay, so she couldn't shout. But she could do something even more satisfying. She grinned just thinking about it.

Jamie looked up from her computer when Grace walked in. "How'd it go?"

"I'll tell you all about it over lunch. First, though, there's something else I need to take care of." Smiling at Jamie's quizzical look, Grace entered her office and gathered up all the files that had to do with Eagleton Energy.

Piling them into her arms, she walked past Jamie's desk and out the door, down the hall, and into Neil Braddock's office. "Is he in?" she said to Cynthia, his secretary.

"Yes."

"Anyone with him?"

"No."

"Good." And then, in one of the most gratifying moments of her life, she marched into Neil's office, dumped the Eagleton Energy files on his desk, bit back a grin at his startled expression, and said, "They're all yours, Neil. I've just given my notice. Enjoy!"

And then, no longer suppressing her grin, she walked out.

That night, when Grace got home, Rose said there was a message for her.

Grace couldn't believe it. Perry had called. And she'd left a number to call back. Grace dumped her briefcase and purse, shed her jacket and called the number.

Perry answered on the first ring. "Oh, Grace, I'm so glad you phoned. I'm sorry I didn't call you yesterday, but I couldn't. I—"

"Doesn't matter," Grace said, interrupting her. "Just tell me where to send the document for you to sign. I'll send it FedEx and include some money so you can overnight it back to me, okay?"

"Okay."

"Unless you've changed your mind again?"

"No, Grace, I haven't changed my mind. I want you to have Emily." She gave Grace the address.

"I'll draw up the document here at home tonight and send it out to you tomorrow morning. You'll have it Wednesday. Remember, you'll have to have it witnessed and notarized, so don't sign it at home. Sign it in front of the notary."

"Okay."

"And, Perry...I'm not sure where I'll be from now on. I'm putting the apartment up for sale and I'm thinking about moving to Seacrest to be near Mom and Aunt Mutt, but I'm not sure when. So if you need to reach me and this number is disconnected, call Mom."

"You're moving to *Florida?*"

"I think so, yes."

"But what about your job?"

"I gave my notice today."

"But why?"

"Because I can't raise a child and keep working at the firm. The hours are horrible. I'd never be here for Emily. Anyway, I'm ready for a change, and I think Seacrest will be a much nicer place for us to live."

"But you love your job, Grace. You told me you thought you'd be made a partner."

"Things change. The partnership went to someone else."

After they hung up, Grace felt bad. She should have told Perry all of it. Especially that not only did things change, but sometimes, even though you didn't first realize it, those changes were for the better.

Both within the family and without, our sisters hold up our mirrors—our images of who we are and of who we can dare to be.

—*Elizabeth Fishel*

CHAPTER 13

"If I were you, Grace, I'd wait until I got settled in Florida before starting adoption proceedings." The speaker was Ellen Forrester, an attorney Grace knew who had handled several private adoptions.

"But why?"

"Well, for one thing, you don't have a job right now."

"But won't I have to wait a period of time before I can apply to adopt in Florida?"

"Nope. They don't have a residency requirement. You can move there on a Friday and start adoption proceedings on a Monday."

"But I really wanted to get this thing settled," Grace said.

"I know, but there's not really any rush, is there? I mean, you've got the document from your sister. She wants you to have the child. And I really think it'll look a lot better for you to have a job when you apply. Otherwise, if you get some cranky old judge, he might just decide to make the adoption provisional, whereas if you're settled with a good income, the judge has the authority to make the adoption final immediately."

Grace sighed. Damn. She hated waiting for *anything*, and she *really* hated waiting for something this important.

"Trust me on this one, Grace," Ellen said. "I know what I'm talking about."

Grace nodded. "Okay. I'll wait." Then she smiled. "Thank you, Ellen. I really do appreciate your help."

"So have your sold your apartment yet?"

"Not yet, but the Realtor called this morning to say she expected two offers today."

"When did you list it?"

"Just last week."

"Wow. That's fast."

"Yes," Grace said. "And Marge—that's the Realtor—said she expected both offers to be good ones."

"So how soon will you move, then?"

"If everything goes all right and we come to an agreement on one of the offers, then I might be able to get out of here by the middle of next month."

They continued to talk about Grace's plans for the duration of their lunch, then said their goodbyes, and Grace headed back to the office. This was her last day to work at the firm, and she knew that there would probably be a going-away party for her this afternoon.

In a way, she felt sad. Finn, Braddock and Morgan had played such a huge and important part of her life for a long time. It would be strange not to go there again after today. But the sadness wouldn't last long, she knew. Because what she had to look forward to was exciting. A bit scary, too, but that was okay. Being a little frightened would add an edge, keep her on her toes.

She was smiling as she entered her building.

"You're gonna have to get a job."

Perry's head shot up and she stared at Don in disbelief. "But who will take care of you if I go out to work?"

"I'm doin' better now," Don said. "Besides, Dale's here at night."

Perry gave him a blank look.

"What're you lookin' at me like that for?" he said in a disgusted tone. "You're a bartender, right?"

"Yes, but—"

"Bartenders work at *night*, right?"

Perry nodded.

"So you can get a job tending bar," he said, enunciating each word slowly, as if he were talking to a two-year-old.

"I'll have to take your car," she said. He hated for her to drive his car unless he was with her. In fact, he held on to the keys and insisted on going wherever she went. She was never sure if it was because he didn't trust her driving or if he thought she might be going out to meet some other guy. Like she would, she thought miserably. Didn't he know she'd never cheat on him?

"Yeah, well, we'll see." He drained his beer and tossed the can toward the trash bin. It missed and fell to the floor.

Perry got up and put the can in the trash. She walked back to the table and sat down again. "I thought you said you had enough money to last us until you could go back to work."

He glared at her. "Quit thinking. You're not good at it."

Perry bit her lip. Why did he always have to say such ugly things to her? "I just thought—"

His pale blue eyes blazed with an emotion Perry didn't want to identify. "I told you. Don't think! Just do what I tell you to do."

For just a moment, Perry actually considered getting up and telling him to go to hell. Grace would have. Grace would never let a man talk to her the way Don talked to Perry. But even the thought of telling him off made her stomach feel queasy. She knew what would happen if she did. He'd turn real ugly, and he wouldn't talk to her except to say something horrible for days. What was wrong with her that she couldn't keep a man happy? And why did she so desperately need a man, anyway?

"W-when do you want me to start looking for a job?" she finally said.

"Tomorrow."

Perry took a deep breath. "All right. I'll check the ads in tomorrow morning's paper. And I'll call Digger's, the bar where I used to work." She'd been wondering about

Digger's, wishing she could drop in and say hi to Andy, the cook, and Steve Digby, who owned the bar. But she'd known better than to suggest going there to Don.

When he didn't answer, she got up and walked to the fridge. "You hungry? Want me to warm up some of that spaghetti we had last night?" Although it was two o'clock, they hadn't had lunch yet. Since neither was working, they usually slept late because Don was a night owl and stayed up half the night, so of course, he wanted her to stay up, too. And when they finally *did* get to bed, he almost always wanted sex.

Perry winced, thinking about the sex. Lately Don had been hurting her. He'd taken to squeezing her nipples harder and harder, and sometimes he bit her, and a couple of times he'd insisted on spanking her. When she'd said she didn't like it, that he was hurting her, he'd gotten mad. He said doing those things was a turn-on for him, and if she really loved him, she'd let him do whatever he wanted to do. He said real women *liked* rough sex, that it turned them on, too. Perry didn't think he was right, but maybe he was. She also hated that his brother Dale could probably hear them. Sometimes she wondered what he was thinking. The past few days he'd been acting funny, and she had a feeling he was tired of having them there, though it hadn't even been two weeks.

She wished she could talk to Grace. Tell her the things Don said and did. But she pretty much knew what Grace would say. And Perry wasn't sure she was ready to be strong and brave and strike out on her own. Even the worst day with Don was better than the best day by herself.

So right now, she was stuck.

It's gonna get better, though. As soon as that cast comes off, he'll feel better, and he'll treat me better. All I have to do is suck it up until then.

"Yeah, sure," he finally said, "spaghetti sounds good."

Pasting a smile on her face, she said, "Coming right up. And after we eat, if you want to, we can watch one of those movies." Yesterday he'd insisted on renting a couple of X-rated films.

She was rewarded with a real smile, and when he said, "C'mere, gimme a kiss," she knew the worst was past.

At least for today.

Both offers for the apartment were good ones, close to her asking price, but Grace's Realtor still advised her to counter.

"They'll both come up, Grace," she said. "People never offer as much as they're prepared to pay. You know that."

So they countered, and sure enough, both offers came back with an increase. In the end, Grace sold the apartment for almost twenty thousand more than she'd hoped to get. Very pleased, she decided that twenty thousand would be put toward a new car.

Grace had never owned a new car. In fact, she hadn't owned any car at all since she'd gone to work at the firm. A person really didn't need a car in Manhattan, and even though a lot of city dwellers owned cars so they could escape to the country on weekends, Grace wasn't one of them. Why have a car for weekend jaunts when you worked every weekend?

The closing was scheduled for the first week of May, and after that, she and Emily would be free to go.

Excited, and needing to tell someone her good news, she called Sal.

"That's great, Grace. And you've definitely decided on Seacrest, huh?"

"Yes. I still have some reservations, but overall, I think it's a good decision."

"I do, too. Maybe you and Mom'll end up good buddies."

Grace laughed. "Dream on. Frankly, I'll be happy if she just puts the sword away."

"You called her yet?"

"You mean today?"

"Yeah."

"No, not yet." Why hadn't she? Was it because she still wasn't absolutely sure she was going to Florida? Or was it because she didn't want her mother to say anything to spoil this day?

"You'll come out and see us again before you leave, won't you?" Sal asked.

"Absolutely."

"Next Sunday is Julie's birthday. Why don't you come then?"

Grace smiled. "It's a date."

"Talk to Jen before you buy Julie anything, though. I think she gave Jen a list."

Grace laughed. "I'm sure she did."

"And don't spend too much money. She's spoiled enough."

"I won't."

They talked awhile more, then Grace said she'd better go. She heard Emily stirring and needed to check on her.

"Okay. See you next weekend. Oh, and Grace?"

"Yes?"

"Call Mom tonight."

Grace thought about her brother's advice all the while she changed Emily and fed her and bathed her and got her ready for bed. By then it was after nine, and she told herself it was too late to call now.

That's ridiculous, and you know it. Mom and Aunt Mutt stay up till at least eleven.

At nine-thirty, she gave in and placed the call.

"Oh, Grace, that's wonderful!" her mother said when Grace told her about the sale of the apartment. "So you're really coming."

"Yes, I guess I am."

"I'm so glad. Mutt and I talk about you and Emily all the time. It's going to be so nice to have you here."

Grace hoped so. She hoped she wasn't making a mistake.

"I know we haven't always seen eye to eye in the past," her mother continued.

That was an understatement, Grace thought wryly.

"So I wanted to reassure you that I'll try hard not to interfere or to boss you around."

"I appreciate that."

"Well, good. So when do you think you'll actually come?"

"I'm not sure yet. It depends on whether we close on time and when the movers can come. Plus I have to buy a car."

"Oh, you're going to *drive?*"

"Well, of course I'm going to drive. What did you think I'd do?"

"I thought you'd fly down. I mean, Grace, you've hardly driven the past ten or fifteen years."

More like twenty, Grace thought. Still, it irritated her that less than five minutes after saying she wasn't going to interfere or boss Grace around, her mother was already trying to do just that. "It's like sex, Mom. Once you do it, you don't forget how."

"Oh, Grace, honestly!"

Grace grinned. "Let's not argue, okay? I'm buying a car, loading it up and driving myself and Emily to Florida. I'm actually looking forward to that. It'll be fun to see some of the places along the way."

"Well, if you really think—"

"It'll be fine, Mom," Grace said through gritted teeth. She could hear her mother sigh. "But you will call when you have a definite day for leaving, right?"

"Right."

After they'd hung up, Grace just shook her head. Her mother would never change. Maybe the move to Florida wasn't such a great idea, after all.

PART TWO

Seacrest, Florida

My sister taught me everything I really need to know,
and she was only in sixth grade at the time.

—*Linda Sunshine*

CHAPTER 14

Grace stretched and surveyed the kitchen of the small
house a friend of her aunt's had found for her. She had just
finished unpacking the last of the dishes and was thinking
about making some iced tea to have while she finished
figuring out where she was going to put everything.

She and Emily had moved in two days earlier, and
already the little house was beginning to feel like home.
Unable to resist, Grace opened the screen door and walked
out onto the back patio. The feature that had completely
sold her on this house was the fenced backyard. Seeing it,
she had immediately envisioned a swing set and sandbox,
a filled baby pool and a dog. She saw herself sitting on the
patio with a glass of lemonade or iced tea while she
watched Emily playing with a cute little puppy.

A Hallmark family, she'd thought with a chuckle. Who,
in her old life, would have ever believed that Grace Campisi,

the ferocious lawyer who invoked fear in the hearts of strong men, would be turned into putty by a little girl?

As Grace came back into the kitchen, that same little girl made waking-up sounds. Grace smiled and headed toward Emily's bedroom.

"Well, hello there, pumpkin," she said.

Emily, who was standing in the crib bouncing up and down, turned at the sound of Grace's voice. As Grace approached the crib, Emily said, "Uh, uh, uh!" and let go of the crib rail. She promptly lost her balance and plopped back down onto her bottom. For a moment, she scowled and looked as if she were going to cry.

"You didn't hurt yourself, silly," Grace said, making a monkey face.

Emily laughed.

Grace laughed with her. Oh, she loved this kid. Reaching into the crib, she drew the warm baby into her arms and kissed her.

"Boy, you're getting heavy." At seven-and-a-half months, Emily now weighed almost fifteen pounds, and Grace could definitely feel the difference when she held her for any period of time, because her arms would start to ache. "I've gotta get into better shape," she muttered as she put Emily down on the changing table to check her diaper. Once she'd changed the baby, she carried her into the kitchen, installed her in the high chair and gave her a hard baby biscuit to chew on—Emily now had two teeth—while she heated a jar of mixed vegetables and opened another of plums, two of Emily's favorite baby foods.

On Monday Emily would start going to the child-care center Grace had found. It was a fantastic place, and Grace knew she was lucky to have gotten Emily in. She'd been on the waiting list for a month, and now they had an opening. It couldn't have come at a better time, because Grace had just been notified that she'd passed the Florida bar.

She'd enjoyed the past few months of not working. It had been nice to be able to relax, take Emily to the beach, visit with her mother and aunt and just have some fun, something she'd never had the luxury of doing before. Luckily, another friend of her aunt's had been willing to rent Grace a small garage apartment until she'd found a house to buy, which had been ideal for her and the baby.

Last month Grace had also started doing volunteer work at a local women's shelter, the Sanctuary.

When she'd first seen the place, she had begun thinking about Isabelle Frank again and how the lawyer had become an advocate for women and their legal problems. That idea excited Grace, and she'd known working at the center was a good starting place for her.

It had turned out to be extremely satisfying on several levels, not the least of which was her budding friendship with the director, Meg Rupert. Grace hadn't had a close woman friend in years; she'd almost forgotten how nice it was to have a contemporary to talk to.

Child care hadn't been a problem because Meg had

told her on the very first day she could just bring Emily along with her. The few times she'd needed to be unencumbered, her mother and aunt had been only too delighted to babysit.

Now the only things left to do were to find some office space where she could set up a practice and finally get the adoption proceedings started.

"And then you'll be mine officially, won't you, sweetie?" she said to Emily, who responded by slapping the spoonful of plums Grace held out and sending the fruit shooting in several directions. One splotch landed on Grace's nose, and she started to laugh. "You stinker. You like doing that, don't you?"

"Da da da," Emily said, grinning her enchanting, dimpled grin. Now she was slapping the tray.

"Ma ma ma," Grace said. "There's no dad here." She knew Emily wasn't trying to say *dad*. She was simply making sounds the way all babies do. Still, Grace might as well try to teach her what *she* wanted her to say.

After Emily's lunch was finished, Grace cleaned her up and carried her into the living room, where she put her in the playpen. With the baby happily occupied with her stuffed animals and toys, Grace hurried back to the kitchen. She wanted to finish putting the dishes away, then she and Emily were going to her mother's.

"Come here, lovey," Grace's Aunt Mutt said an hour later, reaching out to take Emily before Grace's mother could. "Oh, aren't you a beautiful girl?" she cooed. "She looks so cute, Grace. That's an adorable outfit."

"Isn't it?" Grace said. "I couldn't resist it."

The baby wore a red-and-white striped pinafore with matching bonnet. A huge strawberry adorned the skirt and a band of small strawberries decorated the bonnet. Little red socks and white sandals completed Emily's costume.

"It may be adorable, but it sure is skimpy," her mother said. "I hope she's going to be warm enough in this air-conditioning."

"She'll be fine," Grace said.

Mutt took off the bonnet and Emily's black curls sprang free. "Just like your momma's hair," she murmured. "You'll have the devil of a time keeping the knots out when she gets older, Grace."

"I already do. And she *hates* having her hair brushed. I tell you, the kid has a mind of her own."

"Now *that's* a trait she inherited from her aunt."

"Which one?" Grace said, laughing. "You? Or me?"

Mutt grinned. "Who did you think I meant?" Her face sobered. "Perry called yesterday."

"Oh? Did you give her my new number?"

"We weren't here when she called. We were down in the rec room playing bridge." Both Mutt and Grace's mother were avid bridge players. "We would have called her back, but she didn't leave a number. Said she was calling from a pay phone."

"I didn't know they still had those anymore," Grace said. "I wish she'd get a cell phone."

"Not everyone can afford a cell phone," Stella said defensively.

Grace decided it would be best to ignore the comment. Her mother would defend Perry no matter what she did.

Mutt had gone back to exclaiming over Emily, and Emily was smiling, just as if she understood the compliments. Maybe she did, Grace thought. She certainly understood the admiring tone of voice.

"You've had her long enough, Mutt," Grace's mother said. "It's my turn."

"Oh, come on, Stella, you *always* get to hold her," Mutt said. She buried her face in Emily's neck and blew a raspberry. The baby laughed and blew one back.

"Honestly, Aunt Mutt, she doesn't need to learn any more bad habits," Grace said. "She's learning plenty on her own."

"This perfect child?" Mutt said. "I don't believe it."

"What bad habits?" Stella said, frowning at Grace. "She's only seven months old, you know."

"Seven and a half," Grace corrected. "Anyway, I was only kidding. Although—" She laughed. "I'm afraid she's going to have a strong will. Today she slapped a spoonful of plums right out of my hand. Plums went everywhere."

"Oh, you naughty girl," Mutt said, tickling the baby's tummy.

"Oh, for heaven's sake, Grace, she's too young to know

she shouldn't do that kind of thing," Stella said. "I hope you're not going to expect her to be perfect."

"I know that, Mom. I—"

As if Grace hadn't spoken, her mother continued, saying, "After all, not everyone can be like you, Grace. Some of us make mistakes."

Grace slowly turned to look at her mother. "Why are you picking on me, Mom?" she asked quietly. "Does it pain you *that* much to know that I'm going to be Emily's mother instead of your precious Perry?"

Everything went still. Even Emily seemed to freeze at Grace's words.

"I, uh, think I'll take Emily downstairs and show her off," Mutt said. So saying, she got up and quickly left the apartment.

"That wasn't a nice thing to say, Grace," her mother said. Tears shone in her eyes.

"I'm sorry." But Grace wasn't sorry. She was sick and tired of being a scapegoat when it came to Perry. Upset, not just with her mother, but with herself, she walked over to the sliding glass doors that led out to the little private terrace. From this vantage point, she could just see the diamond-bright waters of the Gulf off to the right. She told herself to calm down.

"I just don't know why you'd say such a thing," her mother persisted.

Grace didn't turn around. "Isn't it obvious?"

"No. It's not. Why, I'm the one who *begged* you to

keep the baby. I *never* wanted you to give her to someone else to adopt."

Grace finally turned to face her mother. "That's not the same as wanting me to be her mother. You just wanted me to keep Emily so that if Perry changed her mind it wouldn't be too late."

"That's not true."

"It *is* true. Why won't you admit it? Hell, Mom, I've always known how you feel about Perry. And how you feel about me." She couldn't help the bitterness that had crept into her voice.

"Please don't swear at me, Grace."

Grace rolled her eyes.

"If you think I love Perry more than I love you, Grace, you're wrong. I love all my children equally. But Perry needs me. And you don't. The only one you ever needed or wanted was your father." A lone tear trickled down her mother's cheek, and she brushed it away.

"Is *that* what you think?"

"I don't just think it. I know it. Why, when you were little, you didn't even like me to hug you. You were always pushing me away. Then you'd run to Sal. But Perry was different."

Grace bit her lip. There was some truth to what her mother said. She *had* always preferred her father.

"I—I don't mean to criticize you. I do love you, Grace, and I'm very happy that you've decided to adopt Emily. I think you'll be a wonderful mother." Stella took a long, shaky breath. "Probably a much better mother than Perry could ever be."

Grace was stunned. "Do...do you mean that?"

"Yes, of course, I mean it. I wouldn't say it if I didn't."

When Mutt and Emily returned fifteen minutes later, Grace and Stella were holding hands, sitting side by side on the sofa, and talking softly.

Mutt smiled. "I see you two have settled some things."

Grace's mother smiled, her green eyes resting on Grace's face. "We have. Things we should have settled a long time ago."

Grace squeezed her mother's hand and felt a return pressure.

"Of course," Stella said, her eyes twinkling, "that doesn't mean I won't exercise a mother's prerogative and give my possibly unwanted advice in the future."

Grace grinned. "And that doesn't mean I won't get bristly about it, either." She winked at her aunt. "Leopards don't change their spots overnight."

Stella gently withdrew her hand from Grace's and stood. "All right, you've had that baby long enough. It's my turn now."

As Grace watched her aunt hand over Emily, she thought that this might be the first time in her adult life that she truly felt close to her mother. And it was all Emily's doing. Her advent into their lives had changed everything, and all the changes were for the better.

And they had Perry to thank.

Perry, the perennial screwup, hadn't screwed up this time. In fact, in giving up her daughter, she'd done something wonderful.

I'll never do anything to make her regret her decision, Grace vowed. *And I'll make sure she's always a part of Emily's life.*

Sisters are for sharing laughter and wiping tears.
                                            —*Author Unknown*

CHAPTER 15

Perry wiped down the bar while Angie, the bar's lone waitress, dried glasses. It was two-thirty. The bar had closed a half hour ago.

Perry dreaded going home. Don had been on a tear lately, mainly because he'd been out of work for weeks. And even though she was the one bringing in money and hadn't had anything to do with him not having work, he seemed to blame her for everything that had gone wrong in their lives.

Since April, they'd moved three times. After his brother Dale had told them they'd have to leave, they'd moved in with a friend of Don's because they hadn't had enough money to put a deposit on an apartment. Besides, with neither of them working, they wouldn't have been able to get into one, anyway. Who'd rent to people with no income?

Perry had finally gotten a job the end of April, but it wasn't a very good one. Unfortunately, at the time, Digger's hadn't had an opening. The job she'd managed to find was at a cheap joint featuring a couple of sorry-looking pole dancers. Perry had hated the place. It had made her feel dirty to be there, but she hadn't dared quit. Even though she wasn't making a lot, at least they had *some* money.

By the middle of May, Don's friend had been fed up with them, too, and pretty soon they'd been out on the street again. That was when they'd moved into a sleazy motel where they'd stayed for six weeks. Six horrible weeks that Perry hoped would never be repeated. She still shuddered when she remembered the cockroaches, the stained toilet and tub and the bed that sagged in the middle. Not to mention the beefy landlord who gave her the creeps when he looked at her.

But Don had at last recovered from his accident and had managed to get sporadic construction work, and they'd managed to put enough money together to move into a one-bedroom apartment in a run-down complex in a seedy area of the city. They still didn't have much furniture because Perry's credit was shot and Don's credit cards were maxed out. Even so, the apartment was tons better than the motel.

But now Don was out of work again. Seems he'd gotten into an argument with the foreman on his last job and had ended by hitting the guy, who had promptly fired him.

Thank God Digger's had finally had an opening a few weeks ago, and Bill Winters, who had bought the place from Steve Digby, had called her. It was a miracle he'd found her, for she and Don still didn't have a phone—with their credit problems they would've had to put several hundred dollars down as a deposit, and they didn't have several hundred dollars. But Bill had tracked her down through Angie, who had known where she was working.

"You girls almost done?" Bill asked, walking in from his office in the back.

"Just finishing up," Angie said with a smile. They both liked Bill, a fatherly type with several daughters of his own—the oldest about Angie's age of thirty.

"Can you give me a ride home?" Perry asked Angie. Don wouldn't let her take the car this afternoon, insisting he needed it to "look for work."

Angie hesitated. Perry knew she didn't like driving in Perry's neighborhood.

"I'll drop you off," Bill said.

Perry smiled gratefully. He was such a sweetheart. He reminded her of her dad, even though Sal Campisi had been a thin, wiry man and Bill probably outweighed him by fifty pounds. But Bill had the same caring nature as Perry's dad, and he made her feel safe.

They didn't talk on the way to her apartment. But it wasn't an uncomfortable silence. When they got there, Bill insisted on walking her to the door.

"No, you don't have to," she said.

"I'll just make sure you get inside safely," he said firmly.

His concern nearly brought tears to Perry's eyes. Why couldn't she fall in love with someone nice like Bill? Why did she always go for guys who hurt her?

She wondered what Grace would say if she knew how

Perry's summer had gone. But thinking of Grace only made Perry feel guilty. She hadn't talked to her sister since June because she knew Grace would ask questions Perry didn't want to answer. Instead she called her mother, who never asked those hard questions—probably because she preferred *not* to hear the answers.

I'm such a loser, Perry thought yet again. *If I had any guts at all, I'd leave Don and try to get my act together. But I don't…and I never will have.*

The apartment was dark. Don wasn't home. Oh, God. That probably meant he'd show up stinking drunk.

But she didn't let on what she was thinking and feeling. She didn't want Bill worrying about her. She wasn't his responsibility.

So she thanked him, said good-night and, taking a deep breath, let herself into the empty apartment.

On Thursday, after leaving Emily in the care of her mother and her aunt, Grace headed to the office of Craig Mancuso, an attorney who had been recommended to her by a colleague in New York. She'd called earlier and was lucky to get an appointment for twelve-thirty.

His office was located on the second floor of the First National Bank Building in downtown Seacrest. Grace climbed the stairs—she wasn't getting enough exercise now that she drove everywhere—and walked down the hall to suite 215.

A pretty redheaded receptionist greeted her with a

friendly smile. "Hello. You must be…" She looked at her calendar. "Grace Campisi?"

"Yes."

"Mr. Mancuso's on the phone right now. Have a seat. As soon as he's off, I'll tell him you're here. Would you like some coffee?"

"No, thank you. I'm fine." Grace looked around the small reception area. The receptionist was well-spoken and dressed smartly, the carpeting and furniture were good quality and the magazines fanned across the coffee table were recent issues. Craig Mancuso was obviously doing well.

A few minutes later, the receptionist picked up her phone and spoke softly into the receiver. Hanging it up, she rose, saying to Grace, "Mr. Mancuso will see you now, Miss Campisi." She opened the inner office door and ushered Grace inside.

The fiftyish man who stood behind an oversize walnut desk was tall, trim and distinguished-looking, with thick brown hair going gray at the temples and bright blue eyes behind steel-rimmed glasses. He looked like a professor, except he wore a well-cut and expensive-looking gray pin-striped suit paired with a white shirt and burgundy tie, which no professor Grace had ever known could have afforded.

Grace was glad she'd worn a businesslike black summer-weight pantsuit, even though it was a humid day in the eighties. Her one concession to the heat had been to twist her hair up off her neck and secure it with a wide silver clip.

After the ritual greetings, the secretary—whom

Mancuso had called Kitty—brought them each a glass of ice water and then left them alone.

"So what can I do for a fellow Italian, Miss Campisi?"

Grace smiled. "And a fellow lawyer."

"Oh? Really? Licensed here in Florida?"

"Yes, just recently." Grace explained her situation.

"And Steve Holloway referred you to me?"

"Yes."

"Steve's a good guy. Did you work with him?"

"We were A.D.A.s together in Manhattan, back when we first passed the bar."

"And you've spent the last fifteen years at Finn, Braddock and Morgan?"

"Fourteen and a half," Grace corrected.

He smiled. He had a nice smile, one that extended to his eyes. Grace liked him. He inspired immediate trust, and she thought she would have liked him even if Steve Holloway hadn't given him such a glowing recommendation.

"Okay," Craig Mancuso said. He leaned back in his chair, tenting his hands under his chin. "Here's what I recommend. I'll warn you that you probably won't like it."

Grace frowned. Now what?

"I think you should wait just a bit longer before you do anything about adopting your niece."

"But why? I've already waited longer than I wanted to, and I want my custody of Emily to be legal. I don't like having something so important in limbo."

"I understand how you feel, but you have to be smart

about this. I've handled quite a few private adoptions in the county, and a couple of our family-court judges are real sticklers who want every *I* dotted and every *T* crossed."

"I thought every *I* *was* dotted, Mr. Mancuso."

"Please. Call me Craig."

Grace smiled. "Only if you'll call me Grace."

"Grace it is. Okay, the first problem I see is that you're still technically unemployed. You may have passed the Florida bar and you may have had a big job in New York, but here in Florida, you have no steady source of income."

Grace started to say something, but he held his hand up.

"There's more," he said. "Let me ask you something. The birth certificate says 'father unknown'?"

"Yes."

"*Is* the father unknown?"

"My sister said the father's a sailor. I don't think she knew his last name."

"So he's not totally unknown."

"Well, no," Grace admitted reluctantly.

"The judge might ask this same question." His blue eyes pinned hers. "And you'd be bound to answer truthfully, just as you've answered me now."

Grace nodded.

"If we get one of those two judges I mentioned, they would want to try to find the father before taking your sister's word for it that he's long gone or wouldn't be interested."

Grace sighed.

"Those are the two reasons I recommend waiting. Let's dot as many *I*s and cross as many *T*s as we possibly can before you go to court. In addition to doing something about your job situation, I strongly recommend you contact your sister and see if she *does* know anything else about the father. Why ask for trouble if you can avoid it?"

Grace knew his advice was sound, but she hated the idea of waiting. She'd never been the most patient person in the world, and where Emily was concerned, she felt even more pressure to settle everything now.

"Trust me, Grace, this is the best way to handle things," Mancuso said.

Grace thanked him and said she'd be back when she had talked to Perry again.

Just as she got up to leave, he said, "You've probably already had your lunch today."

Grace tried not to show her surprise at the statement. "Um, as a matter of fact, I haven't."

He smiled. "How about letting me buy you lunch, then? Unless you're in a hurry?"

Grace's mother and aunt were expecting to have Emily all afternoon. In fact, before Grace had left them, her Aunt Mutt had said, "Why don't you make a day of it, Grace? Do some shopping while you're out. Or whatever. We'll enjoy having Emily to ourselves for a while."

"No," Grace said, "I'm not in a hurry."

"Great. We'll go to Piccolo's. Have you been there yet?"

"No. I've seen it, but I haven't tried it." Piccolo's was

on the waterfront, an upscale-looking restaurant that advertised a combination of Italian and seafood specialties.

"They have terrific seafood, plus the best Italian in the city," Mancuso said.

Grace hadn't looked before, but now she glanced at his left hand. No ring. It was hard to believe a man as good-looking and successful as he seemed to be was still single. She wondered if it was by choice. In Manhattan, that wouldn't be at all unusual. Here, though? Of course, Grace might have outdated ideas. Maybe men remained single by choice in small-town America, too.

As they walked through the outer office, Craig Mancuso said, "Kitty, I'm taking Miss Campisi to lunch. I'll be back around two, two-thirty."

When they reached the lobby of the building, he put his hand on her elbow and steered her toward the back. "My car's in the garage."

Grace had imagined they'd walk to the restaurant, which was only a few blocks away.

As if he'd heard her unspoken thought, he said, "Too hot to walk. I don't know about you, but I sweat."

Grace grinned. "Ladies don't sweat. They glow."

His car turned out to be a sleek silver Porsche Carrera convertible. Grace didn't know a lot about cars, but she knew enough to know a Porsche convertible was expensive. Very expensive.

She had to admit, she enjoyed riding through town in an open convertible accompanied by a nice-looking, charming man. *If my friends could see me now...* Then she smiled ruefully. What friends? Who'd had time for friends in her New York life? And she doubted the sensible Meg would be impressed.

Lunch was lovely. The restaurant with its beautifully polished dark wood floors and floor-to-ceiling windows looking out over the sparkling Gulf, the aromas of garlic, tomatoes and basil, the attentive man across the linen-covered table, the delicious food and the smooth wine Craig had ordered—all combined to make Grace wonder if this was some kind of dream. If she'd wake up and find herself back in cold New York, exhausted from another twelve- or fourteen-hour day.

They didn't talk about the adoption. Instead, Craig regaled her with stories about some of his past cases, even telling her about a few mistakes he'd made early in his career. In turn, Grace told him a little about her life in New York. "I never thought I'd be happy anywhere else," she admitted. "But I love it here already."

He smiled. "I felt that way when I first moved here, too."

"When was that?"

The smile faded. "My marriage fell apart when my son died. I couldn't stand it in Miami after that, so I came here."

"Oh, I'm sorry."

"Thank you." He looked away. "We lost Tod ten years ago. But some days it seems like only yesterday."

"What happened?"

"He fell off a mountain. He was in Switzerland,

climbing with his college team and lost his footing. For some reason—I'll never know why—he wasn't connected to the others." He sighed. "He was our only child. Helena had tried for years to get pregnant, finally did with Tod. But we could never seem to have another." He paused, looked out the window. The Gulf looked as if thousands of diamonds had been sprinkled on it. "He was twenty when he died." He swallowed, his Adam's apple moving.

It hurt Grace to look at him. "I am so sorry."

"Yeah," he said with a crooked smile. "Me, too." He made a visible effort to shake off the melancholy that had overtaken him. "Let's talk about something else. Have *you* ever been married, Grace?"

She shook her head. "I was engaged once, in college, but he died in an accident. It took me a long time to get over it. After that, I focused on my career." She smiled wryly. "Less heartache that way."

He reached across the table, laying his warm hand over hers. "So we both have losses in our past."

She nodded slowly. "Yes." She looked at their hands, and she couldn't help thinking how nice it was to be touched in this way.

"I like you, Grace," he said softly.

Her eyes fastened on his. For a long moment, she didn't answer. Then, just as softly, she said, "I like you, too."

"Maybe we could have dinner together sometime."

For once in her life, Grace didn't weigh the pros and

cons before making a decision. Instead, she simply said, "I'd enjoy that."

He squeezed her hand, then let it go.

Grace knew she would think about Craig all day. She'd probably dream about him tonight, too. She wasn't at all sure she was ready for another romantic entanglement, but right now, she wasn't sorry she'd given him the go-ahead.

After all, why not?

She'd risked her heart with Emily, and that had only led to good things. Maybe risking her heart with Craig Mancuso would bring her more good things.

If your sister is in a tearing hurry to go out and cannot catch your eye, she's wearing your best sweater.

—*Pam Brown*

CHAPTER 16

When Grace arrived at her mother's apartment, she found them talking to a visitor.

"Grace," her Aunt Mutt said, "this is Sylvia French. She lives across the hall."

A reed-thin woman with bright red, obviously dyed hair and a hawk-like nose smiled at Grace. "Hello, there. I've heard a lot about you." Her voice was strong, her brown eyes sharp behind glasses with bright red frames. "Your little one certainly is beautiful."

Grace smiled. "Thank you. I think so." Looking at her mother, she said, "Where *is* that little one?"

"Sleeping." Her mother smiled. "I think we wore her out, Grace."

Grace sat down and toed off her shoes. "Ahh, that feels better." She'd worn closed-toe pumps today for the first time since she'd left the firm.

"So how did things go?" her aunt asked.

"Fine," Grace said. She didn't want to talk about what Craig Mancuso had said in front of the neighbor.

Her aunt took the hint and dropped the subject. For a while, the four women chatted about trivial things, then Sylvia French stood. "I'd better be getting home. It was very nice to meet you, Grace. I hope to see you again sometime."

"I'm sure you will," Grace said with a smile.

Once Sylvia was gone, Grace's aunt—always more perceptive than Grace's mother—said, "Now what *really* happened today, Grace?"

Grace sighed and told them how Craig Mancuso had advised her to wait before starting the adoption proceedings and the reasons why. "So now I really have to talk to Perry." She turned to her mother. "Did she give you any idea where we might reach her when she called?"

Stella shook her head. "The only thing she said was they didn't have a phone."

"What about where she's working? Didn't she tell you when she called last month that she'd gotten a job at a bar where she'd worked before?"

"Yes, that's what she said."

"Do you know the name of the place?"

"She never said."

"Why didn't you *ask?*" Grace said in frustration.

"I just didn't think it was important, Grace."

"Not important that we have some way of getting in

touch with her?" Grace knew she sounded critical of her mother, but *damn*, why couldn't her mother be as sensible in her dealings with Perry as she was with everything else?

"I'm not a lawyer like you, Grace," her mother said stiffly.

Oh, shit, now I've hurt her feelings. "I know that, Mom," she said in a softer tone. "And I didn't mean to sound as if I was blaming you, but I'm so *frustrated* with Perry. You'd think she'd *want* us to be able to get in touch with her. What if something happened to you or Aunt Mutt? Wouldn't she want to know? What if something happened to *Emily*, for Chri—for crying out loud?"

"I'm sure she just didn't realize…" her mother said miserably.

It was obvious to Grace that no matter what happened or what Perry did or didn't do, her mother would always make excuses for her.

"Well, the next time you hear from her, please tell her it's urgent that I speak to her, okay?"

Her mother nodded. "Okay."

"Tell her to call me collect if she needs to. At the very least find out the name of the bar where she's working."

"I will."

Grace guessed she'd have to be satisfied with that and just pray that Perry called again soon.

Later that night, as Grace was cleaning up the kitchen after feeding Emily and getting her down for the night, her cell phone rang. The caller ID said Mancuso. Ridiculously pleased, she punched the talk button and said, "Well, hello. I didn't expect to hear from you so soon."

"I've been thinking about you ever since lunch," Craig said.

Something warm slid into Grace's stomach, and her heart began to beat faster. But some remnant of self-preservation kept her from showing how much his remark had affected her.

"I was wondering if I could take you to dinner Saturday," he continued. "I can even recommend a babysitter—a neighbor of mine—a wonderful grandmotherly type."

"My own mother would kill me if I used a babysitter and she found out about it. Let me call and check with her before I say yes. Then I'll phone you back."

"Okay. Here's what I thought. We could drive up to Sarasota—it's only about a forty-five minute drive. There's a terrific restaurant there—out on Longboat Key and they have the most fantastic steaks you ever tasted. Do you like steak?"

"I love steak."

"Good."

When Grace called her mother, there was no hesitation at all. "We'd love to have her, Grace. And you know, Mutt and I were saying we really should buy a portable crib to keep here so that Emily has a proper place to sleep. And a playpen and high chair."

Grace started to laugh. "Mom, where are you going to put all that stuff?"

"There's plenty of room. The crib can go in my bedroom, the high chair in the kitchen and the playpen in the living room."

"That'll make your apartment awfully crowded."

"I don't care. Emily's my *granddaughter!*"

"You could always just come here to babysit."

"That's true, but this way we can go to bed whenever we want to, and you don't have to worry about coming home by any certain time."

"What are you suggesting? That Emily spend the *night?*"

"Why not?"

"But, Mom—"

"Don't you *trust* us?"

"Of course, I trust you. That's not the point."

"Well, what *is* the point?"

"Nothing. Actually, you're right. It makes perfect sense for Emily to spend the night."

"Good," her mother said with satisfaction.

Grace couldn't help the thought that sidled into her mind. If Emily spent the night at her mother's, then Grace would be free to ask Craig in after their date if she wanted to. *Oh, who are you trying to kid? You know you'll want to.* Just thinking about it, Grace felt the stirring of desire. That was what nearly five months without sex would do to a woman, she thought ruefully.

Then again, she didn't want Craig to think she was the

kind of woman who went to bed with a man on a first date. By the next morning, she'd made up her mind that no matter how attracted to him she was or how much she might want to, sex with Craig would have to wait awhile. She needed to get to know him better before she committed to a physical relationship.

Despite this decision, she was really looking forward to their date and spent a good part of Friday trying to figure out what to wear. After looking through her wardrobe, she realized the only thing even remotely suitable was a sleeveless black dress she'd had for ages.

"C'mon, Emily," she said to the baby, who was happily eating Cheerios, "we're going shopping."

Two hours later, Grace tried on a chic red-and-white print polished cotton sheath the saleswoman assured her looked gorgeous with her black hair. "You're sure it's not too short?" Grace said.

"You have great legs," the woman saiα. "You *should* show them off."

"Now I need shoes, too," Grace said.

"Go to Mitzi's," the saleswoman advised. "It's just down the street."

Several hundred dollars later, Grace headed for home with a pair of red strappy high-heeled sandals and a matching red clutch bag. "I need my head examined," she grumbled. "This money would be a lot better spent on the office space I hope to rent." And yet she wasn't really sorry she'd splurged on the new outfit.

In fact, she couldn't wait to see Craig's reaction Saturday night.

"Have I told you how nice you look tonight, Grace?"

Grace knew she *did* look good. Even though she'd spent more than she should have, the new outfit was immensely flattering. And that morning, she'd even had her hair cut into a short, casual style that made her feel younger and, she hoped, softened her face, which she knew was too thin. She grinned. "No, you haven't, but it's never too late."

He laughed. "Well, you do. In fact, you look fantastic."

"Thank you. You look pretty good yourself."

Craig wore light gray slacks, a black silk open-necked shirt and a black linen jacket.

They were now on their way back to Seacrest. Craig had put the top down as they'd left the restaurant, and Grace—who'd anticipated just that—put on the chiffon scarf she'd tucked into her purse. Craig had a Bonnie Raitt CD playing, something soft and sexy and romantic. Grace felt pleasantly full of good food and wine and wished the evening could go on forever.

But all too soon, he was pulling into her driveway. When he got out and came around to open her door, Grace knew she was going to invite him in. Just for a nightcap, she told herself. Just because the evening had been so lovely and he'd shown her such a good time.

So when they reached the front door, she said, "Would you like to come in for a bit? I have some good brandy."

In the moonlight, his eyes gleamed. "Sounds good."

Grace had left one lamp on in the living room because she hated coming home to a dark house. Inside the foyer, she laid her purse and scarf on the little antique table she'd bought a few weeks ago at a flea market and said, "Why don't you go on into the living room and make yourself comfortable? I'll go get us some glasses."

"Grace..." He reached out, grabbing her hand.

She held her breath as he drew her to him.

"I don't really want any brandy," he said, his voice husky.

"Y-you don't?"

He shook his head. He let her hand go and put his arms around her instead. "What I want is you."

And then he kissed her, and Grace was very glad Emily was at her mother's because she knew they weren't going to stop with one kiss.

She might be making a mistake, and she might be sorry in the morning, but right now, she didn't care.

Husbands come and go, children come and
eventually they go. Friends grow up and move away.
But the one thing that's never lost is your sister.

—*Gail Sheeny, from* Sisters

CHAPTER 17

Grace arrived at the daycare center Monday morning,
her stomach queasy at the thought of leaving Emily. In-
tellectually, Grace knew Happy Hearts was a wonderful
facility and she was lucky to have gotten Emily in. Still,
her stomach tightened as she handed the baby to Lisa
Paransky, the director.

Emily, however, didn't seem to have any such qualms.
When Lisa smilingly introduced her to the rest of the staff
and the other babies, Emily immediately wanted to join
the two babies about her age and hardly noticed when
Grace said goodbye.

Grace knew it was ridiculous to feel hurt. She should
be ecstatic that Emily was so obviously going to be
content there.

Her plan for the day was to spend the morning at the

Sanctuary and the afternoon looking at office space. She hoped to settle on something by the end of the day. She was anxious to get her office open and some money coming in so that at least one of Craig's concerns regarding the adoption would be taken care of.

The thought of Craig brought a smile to her face.

He was wonderful. Maybe not as accomplished in bed as Doug had been, but he brought something even better to their lovemaking—a sweetness and the sense that he cared for her, that it wasn't just a roll in the hay for him.

When they'd parted on Saturday night he'd told her he'd call her this week and he hoped they could do something together over the coming weekend. He'd even said they could go to the beach and take Emily. She couldn't help comparing him to Doug yet again. The last thing she could ever imagine Doug doing was offering to take Emily anywhere.

That's one of the reasons you broke things off with him, wasn't it?

She was still thinking about Craig and all the changes in her life when she pulled into the parking lot of the shelter ten minutes later.

The Sanctuary wasn't anything like she'd imagined a women's shelter would be. Instead of an impersonal brick building, it was located in a large Victorian house with a wraparound porch that sat on a corner lot a block away from Seacrest's main business center. An enormous palm tree stood on one side of the front lawn, its fronds swaying in the ever-present breeze blowing in from the Gulf.

There the similarity to an ordinary home ended. For the Sanctuary had bars on all the first-floor windows and secure locks on every door, and at night, there was an armed security guard on the premises. The only way a person could gain admittance was to ring the buzzer and identify themselves. When Grace had made her initial visit, Meg had explained how careful they had to be.

"We've had some irate husbands and boyfriends trying to get in," she'd explained. "Of course, you can't guard against someone who's really nuts—I mean, we can't imprison the women—but we take every precaution, and our local police are good about patrolling past the house periodically."

Grace had nodded her understanding. She well remembered her days as an A.D.A. People did crazy things when they were desperate. Or enraged.

Walking up the three shallow steps to the porch, she rang the buzzer. When Lily, the housekeeper, answered, she said, "Hi, Lily. It's Grace."

A moment later, she heard the click of the lock releasing and she let herself in. The main office was to the left of the entrance, and she could see Meg seated behind her desk.

"You're positively glowing," Meg said as she entered the office. "You must have had a great weekend."

Grace grinned. "I did."

"So come on, tell all. Who is he?"

"What makes you think there's a man involved?"

Meg rolled her eyes. "I've never known any woman to have that look on her face unless she was thinking about a man."

Grace laughed. "Okay, you're right. I had a date Saturday night and it was wonderful and I've been thinking about him ever since."

"You lucky dog," Meg said enviously. "Want to tell me about him?"

"I met him last week. He's the lawyer who's going to handle Emily's adoption."

"Craig Mancuso, you mean?"

"Yes. Do you know him?" Well, of course, Meg probably *did* know him. Seacrest was a small town.

"Yes," Meg said slowly. "I know him quite well, as a matter of fact. We're both on the hospital district board. Plus he handled a couple of cases involving women who were living at the shelter at the time."

"Well? What do you think of him?"

"He's very nice, and he has a good reputation. But, Grace…"

Grace frowned at the look on Meg's face. "What?"

"You do know he's married."

"No, he's not. He's divorced." When Meg said nothing, Grace said, "*Isn't* he?"

Meg shook her head. "As far as I know, he and his wife are only separated."

"But, he said—" Grace stopped abruptly. She thought

back to their conversation over lunch the day they'd met. *My marriage fell apart,* he'd said. He'd never actually said the word *divorced.* Suddenly, she felt cold. *Was* he still married?

"I'm sorry, Grace. It's really none of my business."

"Don't worry about it, Meg," Grace said, regret and disappointment settling like a stone in her heart. "I'm glad you told me. And you're right. I needed to know."

Upset as she felt, Grace knew she had to put the whole Craig issue out of her mind to think about later, when she was alone. Right now she had work to do. Besides, she didn't want Meg feeling bad about telling her.

"You okay?" Meg asked, concern etched on her face.

"I'm fine." Grace forced a smile. "I'm a big girl. This isn't the first time a man's disappointed me, and it probably won't be the last."

Meg smiled cynically. "It's hell to be a woman sometimes, isn't it?"

"Amen, sister." Grace took a deep breath, made herself sound brisk. "Now, what have you got for me today?"

"I want you to meet someone new. Her name is Anna." At the shelter, they only used first names. Meg had explained this policy was for the protection of the women there. It ensured that none of the staff would ever inadvertently reveal their presence. "She came yesterday with her three children," Meg continued. "She hasn't said much, but it's obvious she's a battered wife."

"Damn," Grace said. "How many does that make?"

"Four this month."

Grace shook her head. Why a woman allowed herself to be physically abused was something she'd never been able to fathom. Oh, she knew some of them felt they had nowhere else to go or they were too afraid to try to get away because the man in their life had threatened them, but it was still difficult for her to grasp because she'd never been dependent on a man. She couldn't help thinking about Perry. Thank God she seemed to have learned her lesson and now, even though she still gravitated toward losers, at least she was no longer someone's punching bag.

"I'll go get her," Meg said. "She won't want to talk in front of the other women."

While Meg was gone, Grace helped herself to some coffee, then sat and waited for her to return with the unknown Anna. A few minutes later Meg, accompanied by a small blond woman, entered the office.

"Grace," she said, "this is Anna. Anna, Grace Campisi, an attorney who works for us."

"H-hello," Anna said softly. Her face had several old-looking bruises and one, just below her eye, that was a horrible greenish-yellow color. There was also a cut on her chin that had started to scab over.

Grace stood. She held out her hand. "Hello, Anna."

Anna seemed taken aback, but then she leaned forward and shook Grace's hand.

Meg invited Anna to sit and, after another hesitation, she perched on the edge of a chair. She reminded Grace of a skittish bird ready for instant flight.

Grace gave her an encouraging smile. "Why don't you tell me what happened that caused you to come to the Sanctuary, Anna?"

Anna bowed her head.

Meg reached over and put a hand on her arm. "It's okay. We only want to help you."

Anna nodded. "I know."

"Go ahead," Meg encouraged. "What you say here is just between us."

"M-my husband drinks," Anna said, so softly Grace had to lean forward to hear her. "He gets crazy sometimes, especially when the kids fight or the baby cries."

"So he hits you," Grace said flatly.

Anna's head jerked up. "It...it isn't his fault. It's my fault. I—I shouldn't say the things I do."

Grace gritted her teeth. This was a familiar refrain. She'd heard it as an A.D.A., she'd heard it from Perry and now she was hearing it at the shelter. "It's *not* your fault. No one has the right to hit you, no matter what you say."

Anna twisted her hands in her lap.

"Does he hit the children?"

Anna nodded almost imperceptibly. "H-he didn't used to, but the other day he twisted Lizzie's arm so hard she screamed." Tears leaked from the corners of her eyes. "I was afraid maybe he broke it, but it seems to be okay now."

"Is that why you left? Because he hurt your daughter?"

"Yes," she whispered.

"Does he know where you are now?"

She shook her head. "No."

Grace sighed. "Do you have any money?"

Anna bit her lip. "N-not much. I—I waited until he went to work—he's on the night shift—then I just packed up what I could carry, grabbed the kids and called a cab and came straight here. I have about a hundred dollars. It was the food money for the rest of the month." She swallowed. "When he finds out I took it, he'll be so mad. H-he scares me when he gets mad like that."

"You don't have to go back," Meg said.

Anna looked at her, her blue eyes too big for her face. "But I can't stay here forever. You said thirty days was the most anyone can be here."

"Yes, I know, but there are other places you can go. Apartments you can rent."

"An apartment? How could I afford an apartment? I don't have a job. And even if I did, where would my kids go? Only Lizzie's in school. Jimmy's only three, and the baby's only six months old."

And Grace had thought *she* had problems. Her life was a piece of cake compared to Anna's. "You can file charges against your husband, and then you can go home," she said.

"F-file *charges?* You mean, like, put him in jail?"

"That's exactly what I mean."

Anna shook her head violently. "No. No, I won't do that. Jake's a good man, he really is. He…he just, he just gets crazy when he drinks."

Grace and Meg exchanged a glance.

"Anna, if you won't file charges, you're tying our hands," Grace said.

"I'm sorry."

For a moment, the three women sat there. Grace was thinking how frustrating it was to deal with a woman who refused to see reality. Anna was thinking it was easy for someone like the smart, good-looking lawyer to say she should file charges, but she didn't know what a good man Jake was down deep. And Meg was thinking that some days she wished she could just throw in the towel and do something easy for a living, like open-heart surgery.

"Why did you come here, Anna?" Meg finally asked.

Anna looked at her. "I—I was scared."

"Do you plan to go back home?" Grace asked.

"I don't know what to do. I just know I can't put Jake in jail. If I do, he'll lose his job. And then what? How will we live?"

"What about family?" Grace asked. "Is there anyone you could go and stay with?"

Anna shook her head. "There's only my brother, but he lives in Ohio." She turned to Meg again. "You're not going to make me leave, are you?"

"Of course not," Meg said. "You can stay the full thirty days, and in the meantime, we'll put you in touch with a couple of organizations we work with. Organizations that can help you financially. We can also talk to your husband, see if he'd be willing to go to counseling on his own—we can arrange free counseling for him *and* you. We'll also encourage him to join AA. There are any number of positive things that *can* happen. I'll also look into some work situations for you."

After Anna left the office, Meg and Grace discussed her situation for a while, then moved on to other things. The morning flew by, and as Grace prepared to leave, Meg said, "Where are you off to this afternoon?"

Grace smiled. "I'm going to go and look at some office space."

"Really? Where?"

So Grace told her.

"Both those places sound as if they'll be expensive."

Grace grimaced. "I know. I was hoping to pay less. But I'm anxious to get my practice going so I can go forward with the adoption." Mentioning the adoption reminded her of Craig and his dishonesty. Damn. She guessed she might have to find another attorney now, too.

"You know," Meg said thoughtfully, "Coralee Wainwright, who's one of our biggest contributors, might be willing to rent out space fairly inexpensively in one of her properties. Want me to talk to her?"

"Where are her properties?"

"She owns those two houses on Orange Blossom Drive. You know—one houses that antique shop downstairs and Dr. Donofrio's offices are on the main floor of the other one. What I was thinking is she might have a vacancy upstairs."

"Those would be *perfect*," Grace said. The street Meg was referring to was charming, with shops and offices intermingled with older homes.

"Let me call her, see if she has anything available."

Grace sat and listened to the one-sided conversation, smiling as Meg gave her a glowing recommendation, ending by saying, "She's been invaluable to us here, Coralee. If we'd had to pay for the help she's given us, it would have cost us a bundle."

When she got off the phone, she was smiling. "She said she's got the ideal space over the antique shop, and she'll make you a good deal if you like it. She said you can go over now, and she'll meet you there."

"Meg, I can't thank you enough."

"Sure you can. Just keep giving us your time free of charge!"

Grace laughed. "You got it."

"You up for a movie over the weekend?"

Since Grace now had no intention of going out with Craig again, she said, "Sure. What did you have in mind?"

"Maybe that new Pierce Brosnan movie at the AMC? And Chinese afterward?"

"If my mother is willing to babysit, it'll be a date. I'll let you know tomorrow."

"Call me after you talk to Coralee, though. I'll be anxious to know if it works out."

Grace promised she would.

The space over the antique shop was perfect for Grace.

Two rooms, one large, one small, both with doors that opened onto a center hallway. Grace would take the largest one as her office and, until she could afford a secretary, use the smaller one for storage.

And when Coralee, who turned out to be a tall and imposing woman of about seventy with white hair, bright red lipstick and a figure most thirty-year-olds would envy, named the rent, Grace couldn't say yes fast enough.

When Grace asked what kind of lease Coralee wanted her to sign, Coralee said, "The standard one-year lease will be fine. I'll have it ready for you tomorrow."

They shook hands and Grace, after giving Coralee a check for the first month's rent and getting a set of keys in return, said she would start setting up shop that week. "I'll need to get some business cards and letterhead right away. Oh, and I'll need a sign. Do you know of a good place?"

"Kelly's Printing over on Second Street," Coralee said. "Tell George I sent you. He'll give you a good deal."

"Thank you. I will."

"I'll be your first client," Coralee said. "I need a new will."

Grace almost said, *But surely you already have an attorney?* She stopped herself in time. No sense in being stupid. If Coralee Wainwright wanted to be her benefactor, who was Grace to question her?

Perry had taken to leaving a portion of her tips at the bar. Bill gave her a zippered money bag she could keep in the safe. He didn't ask her why she wanted it, and she didn't tell him, but she knew he knew. With anyone else, she would have been ashamed, but Bill seemed to understand, and he wasn't judgmental. All he said was "If you need help with anything, you just let me know."

Perry had nodded.

So far she'd accumulated a couple hundred dollars. She decided when she had a thousand, she would leave Don, for she'd finally faced the truth. Their relationship was going nowhere, and she no longer wanted it to.

And then, when she was finally doing something Grace would approve of, she would call her sister.

But not before.

Grace decided she wasn't going to phone Craig and confront him as she'd first thought she would. Instead, she would wait until he contacted her.

He called about nine o'clock Wednesday night.

"Oh, hello, Craig," she said coolly.

"Hi." There was a quizzical note to his voice. "Did I catch you in the middle of something?"

"No. I just put Emily to bed and was getting ready to fix myself a cup of tea." Now that she was actually talking to him, she found herself getting angrier by the minute.

"Wish I was there with you," he said softly.

I'll just bet you do, you lying son of a bitch....

When she didn't answer his comment, he said, "Is something wrong, Grace?"

"You could say that."

When she didn't elaborate, he said, "Let's not play games, okay? Just tell me what the problem is."

"The *problem* is you are still married, Craig. The *problem* is you didn't tell me. The *problem* is you're not the person I thought you were."

"Dammit, Grace, I meant to tell you. I was *going* to tell you. But—"

"But *what?*" she interrupted furiously.

"But I was afraid you wouldn't see me again if you knew."

"You've got *that* right, buster. I don't date married men. And I sure as hell don't have sex with them!" And with that, she slammed down the phone and burst into angry tears.

She was as stupid as Perry. Neither *one* of them had any sense when it came to men. They *both* picked jerks. Grace just picked better-dressed and better-educated jerks.

When the phone rang again, she ignored it. She knew it was Craig calling back, and she didn't want to talk to him right now. In fact, she never wanted to talk to him again.

"Go screw yourself," she muttered, glaring at the phone even as the tears kept coming.

It finally stopped ringing. Grace wearily headed into the kitchen. The cup of tea was no longer tempting. What she really needed was a good strong vodka and tonic, something to anesthetize her, something to take away the pain pressing on her chest. But she didn't have any vodka.

The phone rang again. She glared at it. It kept ringing. Three times. Five times.

She hadn't yet signed up for voice mail, so unless she answered, the phone would continue to ring until the caller gave up. Grabbing it, she pushed the talk button and said, "You're going to wake the baby. Stop calling me. I don't want to talk to you."

"Grace? Is something wrong?"

Oh, shit. It was her mother. "Oh, Mom, I'm sorry. I thought this was someone else."

"Who else?" her mother said in alarm. "Is some pervert calling you?"

"No, no, nothing like that. I—I just had an argument with a…with someone I know…and I don't want to talk to him again tonight."

"With *who*, Grace? I didn't know you knew any men other than that lawyer."

"Look, Mom, I really don't want to discuss this. It's personal. Can we just forget it?"

"But, Grace—"

"I mean it. Let's just forget it. Now tell me why you called. Did you hear from Perry?"

"No, I just wondered how Emily did at day care today."

"She did just fine. In fact, she loved it."

"They probably tell all the mothers that."

"They didn't have to tell me. I could see for myself. She didn't even cry when I left, she was so busy making friends with the other babies."

"I really hate to see her going to day care. I know you think Mutt and I are too old, but we'd really enjoy taking care of her while you work."

Oh, God. She wasn't up for this discussion again. Not tonight. "I told you. She loves it. And it's a wonderful facility. The best in the city. They have a waiting list a mile long. I'm extremely lucky to have gotten her in."

"No matter how nice it is, she's still being cared for by strangers. And being around all those other children, she'll probably catch every bug. Is that what you want for her?"

Grace closed her eyes. "Mom, please…I'm really tired, and I have a headache. Can we talk about this tomorrow?"

After a few seconds' silence, her mother sighed. "I'm sorry, Grace. I know you think I'm bossy and interfering. It's just that Mutt and I love Emily so. And we just want what's best for her."

"I know you do. So do I."

Her mother started to say something else, then obviously changed her mind. "Well…I guess I'll let you go. But I really *do* want to talk to you about this again, okay?"

"Fine."

After that, they said goodbye, and Grace decided the best thing for her to do now would be to unplug the phone, take a couple of Advil and go to bed.

More than Santa Claus, your sister knows when you've been bad and good.

—*Linda Sunshine*

CHAPTER 18

Grace had just mixed up a bowl of rice cereal for Emily when the doorbell rang. She frowned and looked at the kitchen clock. It was only seven-thirty. Who in the world was at her door this early in the morning?

"I'll be right back, sweetie pie."

Emily grinned and hit the high-chair tray. She was always in a good mood when she got up, for which Grace was continually thankful. She couldn't imagine what it would be like to have a cranky baby in the morning. Dropping a kiss on Emily's head, she put a couple of pieces of cut-up banana on the tray—which Emily eagerly snatched—then Grace walked out to the foyer.

Reaching the front door, she looked out the peephole and saw a young blond woman holding an enormous bouquet of roses.

"Grace Campisi?" the woman asked when Grace opened the door.

"Yes."

"These are for you." The woman handed Grace the flowers, then waved goodbye and left.

Grace didn't have to read the accompanying note to know who had sent them. It could only have been Craig. Part of her wanted to pitch the flowers *and* the note into the trash. But the other part, the part that adored flowers, was also curious about what he had to say.

She told herself she would just read the note. That's all. She certainly had no intention of forgiving him or contacting him or anything else.

Tearing open the envelope, she extracted the folded sheet of paper. It read:

Dear Grace,

I know what I did was wrong. I should have told you Helena and I were only separated, not divorced. Like I said, I was afraid you wouldn't see me again if I did. I hope someday you'll forgive me, but if you don't, I can't honestly say I blame you. What I want you to know is that meeting you has shown me I no longer want to live the way I have been—not really married, but not free, either. I intend to go down to Miami this weekend and talk to Helena. It's time we made this seven-year split legal so that we can both go on with our lives.

I would still like to represent you when you are ready to start adoption proceedings for Emily. However, if you feel you'd rather work with someone else, I'll abide by that decision and recommend another attorney.

I am sorrier than you will ever know, Grace. I'll probably be kicking myself for a long time, because you are one terrific woman and from the moment you walked into my office, I felt a connection. I think, if we'd had the chance, we could have had something really special together.

It was signed simply, *Craig*.

Grace sighed deeply. Her anger had disappeared. Now she just felt sad because even if he *did* get a divorce, she was afraid she would never be able to trust Craig again. Maybe that was too harsh, but she couldn't help it. She detested liars.

And yet part of her sympathized and even understood *why* he had lied. Because she'd felt that connection, too.

Carrying the roses back to the kitchen, she dug out a vase, filled it with water and hurriedly arranged the roses. Then she set them in the middle of the table. Emily stared at them, then pointed. "Ooooh," she said.

Grace smiled. "So you like flowers, do you? Such a girlie-girl."

Emily, who had finished the banana, slapped her tray again and continued to ogle the flowers. Grace finished fixing her cereal, then fed her. Before reading the note,

Grace had been determined she wouldn't even acknowl-
edge the flowers, but now she changed her mind.

After cleaning up Emily, she carried her into the living
room and settled her in the playpen. Then she went into
her bedroom and turned on her computer. While it was
booting, she dug out Craig's business card and double-
checked his e-mail address.

When the computer was ready, she opened her e-mail
program and began a new message.

TO: C.Mancuso@seacrest.net
FROM: GMCampisi@zulu.net
SUBJECT: The Flowers
Craig, just wanted to let you know the flowers arrived.
They are gorgeous. Thank you. I will call you when I'm
ready to begin adoption proceedings. I still want you
to represent me.

She debated about whether to say anything concerning
his divorce and finally decided not to. After signing her
name, she pushed Send and the post went off into cyber-
space. She knew Craig would be disappointed in its brevity
and lack of encouragement, but she wasn't ready to think
about the future and whether it might still include him.
Right now she felt she had all she could manage with
building a law practice, raising Emily and dealing with all
the changes in her life.

It had probably been a mistake to go out with Craig to

begin with. But what was done was done, and she didn't intend to waste another minute regretting it.

Perry had gotten so she dreaded the weekends because Don was at his worst then. If only she had enough money saved to move out. But the cost of apartments—even ones as dilapidated as hers and Don's—were so expensive. If she only had a friend who would give her a place to stay for a while. But there wasn't anyone anymore. She and Angie had become close, but Angie was living with her boyfriend in a one-bedroom apartment, so that wasn't an option for Perry.

This situation is all your own fault. If your credit wasn't so bad, you could borrow some money. And if you hadn't mooched off Grace and Mom so many times, you could ask them to help you out.

Perry guessed she'd just have to wait awhile longer. As long as things didn't get any worse than they were now, she figured she could stand it.

Bill now drove her home almost every night because Perry rarely had the use of the car. She took the bus to work or, when Don was around, he drove her, but even if a bus had been available when she got off at night, she never would have gone home on one. Not in her neighborhood.

Perry was thinking all this as she let herself into the apartment Saturday night. She didn't think Don was there because the place was dark, so she was totally unprepared to see him sprawled on the couch when she walked into the living room and snapped on the overhead light.

"It's about time you got home," he snarled.

Perry's heart slammed into her throat. She was no later than normal, but it was obvious he'd been drinking heavily, so there was no sense correcting him. It would just infuriate him more.

He lurched to his feet. "I've been waiting for you."

Perry tried to walk past him, but he grabbed her arm. "Let me go. You're hurting me."

"You been holdin' out on me."

"I don't know what you're talking about."

"Sure you do, you little bitch. I know you're makin' more in tips than you been givin' to me."

"That's not true." Perry knew all she could do was brazen it out. She only hoped she didn't look as scared as she felt. "Business has been slow the past few weeks."

"Lemme see what you made tonight."

She swallowed. She'd actually taken in more than fifty dollars in tips tonight, Friday and Saturday being the busiest nights of the week at Digger's. But she'd put half of it in her secret stash in the safe. Opening her purse, she took out the crumpled bills and coins she'd stuffed inside and gave them to him.

He dropped his grip on her arm and mumbled drunkenly as he attempted to count the money. Perry seized the chance to get away from him and went into the bedroom and closed the door. She considered wedging a chair under the knob, but knew that would only enrage him.

"Where's the rest of it?" he shouted, staggering into the bedroom.

"That's all there is, Don," she said as calmly as she could.

He glared at her. "There's only twenty-eight dollars here. I know you made more than that. Now where is it?"

"I don't have any more. I told you. It was a slow night."

He raised his right fist. "Quit lyin' to me, you bitch!"

Before Perry could react, he swung at her. Because he was drunk, his aim was off, but his fist still connected with her chin.

Perry's head snapped back. Shock froze her for a moment. She touched her chin.

"I'll teach you to lie to me!" he shouted, grabbing her by the shoulders and shaking her.

Perry tried to push him away, but even drunk, he was much stronger than she was. He threw her down on the bed and raised his fist again. Perry threw her hands up to shield her face, but the blow still landed near her left eye. As he drew back to hit her again, she lifted her feet and kicked out as hard as she could. The kick knocked him over, and he landed heavily. Cursing, he began to get up. Perry scrambled off the bed and raced into the living room. Looking around wildly, she searched for something, anything, to keep him away.

There was nothing. Dashing into the minuscule kitchen, she opened the bottom cupboard and grabbed the first thing she saw—a frying pan.

"Don't come near me!" she cried as he lurched into view.

"Bitch," he muttered, but he kept his distance.

For a long moment, it was a standoff—her holding the pan up, him staring at her. Then, still muttering and cursing, he picked up the car keys, which were lying on the floor and slammed out of the apartment.

Damn! If only she'd seen those car keys, she would have left. Now she was stuck here, and no telling what he'd be like when he came back.

Maybe he'll kill himself driving drunk, she thought. No, more than likely he'd kill some innocent person. Or her when he came home.

Walking to the door, she double locked it, although that wouldn't keep him out since he had the keys. Then she went into the bathroom and turned on the light.

Oh, God. Her left eye was already swelling and blood seeped from a cut in the corner. Her chin throbbed, too, and she knew she'd look a mess in the morning.

Maybe she should put ice on it. Isn't that what you were supposed to do for swelling?

If only she had somewhere to go and some way to get there. She'd leave here tonight and never come back. But she didn't, so right now she was stuck.

But come Monday, she was determined she would find a way to leave him. Even if it meant she had to call Grace.

"What happened to your face?"

Perry had known it would be hard to show herself in the bar, but she hadn't realized just how ashamed she would feel when Bill and the others saw her. "I—I ran into a door."

"Bullshit," Bill said. His eyes flashed dangerously. "It's that creep you live with. He hit you."

Perry's eyes filled with tears. Angie, who had just walked into the room from the kitchen, stopped in her tracks. "Perry," she said. "Ohmigod. What happened?"

"That no-good SOB she lives with hit her," Bill said.

Luckily, there were no customers left over from lunch, so the bar was temporarily empty except for the three of them and Carlos, the cook. Perry thought about continuing to try to pretend Don hadn't hit her, but she knew they wouldn't believe her, anyway.

"Oh, Perry," Angie said.

"You're not going back there," Bill said.

"I don't want to," Perry said, "but I have nowhere else to go. And I can't afford to get a place of my own. Not yet, anyway."

"You can stay here," he said.

"*Here?*"

"Yes, I'll clean out the storage room. We'll put a cot in there and something for you to put your clothes in, and you can just sleep here."

Staying at the bar wasn't a bad idea. There was a bathroom and a kitchen. No shower, but Perry could take sponge baths and wash her hair in the sink. That wasn't really a problem. And being at the bar would solve her transportation problem, too. "Oh, Bill, that would be wonderful," she said gratefully. "But I don't have any of my things with me."

"I'll take you home to get them. Angie, you can manage for a while, can't you?"

"Sure, no problem."

"But Don was there when I left," Perry said. She couldn't stand the thought of a confrontation with him.

"Good," Bill said. "I'll have a few things to say to him. And if he causes any trouble at all, we'll call the cops." He looked as if he'd love to do just that.

But when they arrived at the apartment, Don was gone. The place smelled of stale beer and it embarrassed Perry for Bill to see how dirty it was. She'd given up trying to keep it clean because Don constantly sabotaged her efforts. She hurriedly packed her belongings into two duffel bags and a large tote, and forty minutes after they'd gotten there, she was ready to leave.

"Until we can get that storage room fixed up for you, you're coming home with me," Bill said as they drove back to the bar.

"But—"

"Mona won't care," he said, correctly guessing what Perry had been about to say. "Hell, we've got daughters of our own. She knows things can happen."

And he was right. Mona instantly made Perry feel at home, giving her a big hug and saying, "Honey, I'm so glad Bill was there to help you out."

That night Perry slept better than she'd slept in

months. And the next day, she awoke to the smell of bacon and fresh coffee.

"You know, honey," Mona said when Perry came down to breakfast, "Bill and I were talking. We'd be happy to rent you a room here at the house until you can afford to find a place of your own. We don't even use the upstairs now that the girls are gone. In fact, the only time there'd be anyone else up there with you is when the grandkids come to visit."

Perry was afraid she was going to cry. It had been a long time since anyone had been so nice to her. "That would be wonderful," she managed to say. "I—I don't know how I can ever repay you."

"Oh, nonsense," Mona said. "It'll be fun to have a girl around the house again."

"And it'll be a lot safer," Bill said.

After breakfast, Perry showered and changed into clean clothes, then Mona took her around the house, showing her where everything was and how the appliances worked. She even told her she could use their computer if she wanted to. "We can get you a free e-mail account at Yahoo! or someplace like that, if you like."

Perry figured she was the only almost twenty-seven-year-old in the country who didn't have e-mail, so she was thrilled. Maybe now she could keep in regular touch with Grace. And if she ever got her credit straightened out, she might even be able to get a cell phone.

But first things first.

She couldn't take advantage of Bill and Mona's generosity forever. She needed to work hard, save as much money as she could, and figure out how to get a place of her own. And she needed to stay away from men.

She wondered what Don had thought when he'd come back to the apartment and found her gone. He hated to be alone, and she knew he wouldn't be able to pay the rent without her. He would eventually be evicted. Well, that was his problem.

Perry touched her swollen cheek, and though it hurt, she couldn't help but smile.

As far as she was concerned, Don was history.

But that night, history reared its ugly head. It was just before eight when the door to the bar opened and Don walked in. Perry saw him before he saw her. Her heart skidded. Oh, God. She wasn't ready for this.

He looked around, then spied her and walked over to where she was standing behind the bar. "What the hell's going on, Perry?"

Her glance didn't waver, even though her insides were jumping. "Nothing's going on. I moved out, that's all."

"You didn't even leave a note. What was I supposed to think?"

"I didn't think you'd care."

"You need any help here?" Bill said, walking up next to her.

"No, I'm fine. I can handle this," Perry said. She smiled at him. "But thanks."

"Mind your own business," Don snarled.

"When you come into my bar and harass my help, it *is* my business," Bill said, glaring at him.

Don's face turned ugly. "Hey, old man, you don't want to mess with me."

Bill looked at Perry. "Did that sound like a threat to you?"

"Damn right, it's a threat," Don said.

"Don…" Perry said warningly.

"Yeah, tough guy," Bill said, "if I were you, I'd watch it. I'm not a woman. It might not be so easy to take care of me."

"Bill," Perry said, laying a hand on his arm. "Let me talk to him, okay?"

Bill looked as if he wanted to argue with her, but he finally just nodded. "If you need me, just yell."

"I will." When Bill had walked away, Perry said, "Why don't you go home, Don? There's no point in staying, because I'm not coming back."

"Maybe I don't want to go home."

"Well, here's the thing. If you don't leave, I'll tell Bill to call the cops, and when they get here, I'll press charges." She pointed to her eye. "I've still got proof of what you did."

"You bitch," Don said, his face twisting. "Hell, I'll go. I was sick of you, anyway." Cursing, he turned and stomped out.

Perry's stomach didn't settle down until the door had closed behind him.

"Uh-oh, somebody sure was mad," Angie said, coming over and standing next to Perry.

Perry took a deep breath. Her hands were shaking, but

damn, she felt good. In fact, she felt better than she'd felt in a long time.

She could hardly believe it. She had stood up to Don.

It was the first time in her entire life that she'd ever stood up to a man. "He was, wasn't he?" She grinned. "I told him to get lost."

"I'm proud of you."

"I'm proud of you, too," Bill said, walking up to them. "In fact, this calls for a celebration. How about a beer on the house?"

Angie made a face. "Last of the big spenders."

Perry laughed.

Maybe now she could even call Grace.

Grace hung up the phone and sat thinking. She had just talked to Perry and felt really encouraged that her sister was finally getting her life on some kind of positive track. Perry had left Don, and her boss and his wife seemed to have taken her under their wing. Grace was glad. Perry deserved to have some good luck, for a change.

Grace had promised to send Perry some of Emily's pictures via e-mail as soon as Perry had an account of her own. But Perry was too anxious to wait and gave Grace the e-mail address of the bar. "Bill won't mind," she'd said. "And he's got a color printer there."

Grace had promised to send the photos that evening.

The only disappointing part of their conversation concerned Emily's father. Perry had insisted that all she knew about him was his first name. "It was Johnny," she'd said. "I told you everything else I know, Grace."

"But you said you met him through his cousin."

"But I have no idea where his cousin is now. I haven't seen her in two years, Grace."

Grace had sighed.

"Why do you care, anyway?" Perry had asked. "You want Emily, don't you?"

"It's because I want her that I care." Grace had explained what Craig Mancuso had told her.

"But I can't tell you what I don't know."

Grace had finally had to accept that Perry had given her all the information she could. Surely the judge, whomever he turned out to be, couldn't expect what didn't exist.

Could he?

When sisters stand shoulder to shoulder, who stands
a chance against us?

—*Pam Brown*

CHAPTER 19

Throughout the remainder of September, Grace concentrated on getting her practice established. Because of Meg, Grace was invited to speak at the Seacrest Women's Club, which led to invitations to talk to two other women's groups—one at the Catholic church and one at the Methodist church. These appearances brought her half a dozen clients needing wills, divorces and legal advice concerning things like broken contracts and job discrimination.

She also spoke to a gathering of tenants in her mother's apartment building. Afterward, one of the elderly men who lived there approached her. He was worried about his money. He had given his nephew power of attorney over his investments and he was now concerned that the nephew was stealing from him. He wanted to rescind the power of attorney and asked her to help him. His request and the questions of several others in the group made

Grace realize that seniors were as vulnerable as younger women, sometimes even more so. That was the moment she knew she wanted to have two specialties—women and seniors.

The day after her talk at her mother's building, the owner of the building called Grace and asked her to represent them in a contract dispute with their management company. And two weeks after that, Lucinda Fellows, a wealthy resident and friend of her aunt Mutt's, called Grace and asked if she'd be interested in taking over her legal affairs. Grace was very interested and said so—the woman had extensive real-estate holdings as well as substantial shares in several companies. Lucinda promptly put Grace on a monthly retainer, which was enough to cover the rent on Grace's office.

Grace could hardly believe it, but by the end of October, she had nearly a full caseload, having picked up three more clients from an article about her that ran in the *Seacrest Sentinel*. The feature story was also due to Meg's influence, and Grace laughingly said she was going to have to give Meg a percentage of her fees if she kept sending her clients.

"Oh, don't worry," Meg replied. "I'll get repaid in spades. I'm going to take it out in pro bono work for the shelter." Then she smiled. "Seriously, Grace, I'm happy for you. And believe me, my motives are entirely selfish. You're a valuable addition to our staff at the Sanctuary, and I wanted to ensure that you'll stay in Seacrest."

"Thank you, Meg. I'm grateful."

Emily, too, thrived during this period. She grew two inches, gained several pounds and now had four teeth. By the end of October she could stand unaided and was even attempting to take a step or two. Grace knew that any day now the baby would walk, and she kept her new digital camera ready at all times to capture the milestone so that Perry and her mother and aunt could share the moment, too.

Grace knew she was prejudiced, but with her thick black curls, gorgeous slate-blue eyes and deep dimples, Emily was beautiful enough to be a baby model. Grace actually thought about checking into it, then decided she had enough on her plate without adding anything else. She took lots of pictures of Emily, though, and had several of the nicest ones framed for home, for the office, for her mother and aunt and, of course, for Perry.

The sisters were now in weekly contact via e-mail. Grace tried to keep Perry up to date on Emily's progress and anything else that she thought might interest her sister. Perry wasn't the world's best correspondent, but Grace gave her an A for effort. But even Perry's short posts with their limited information were a lot better than her past silences. And she was making progress. In her latest e-mail, she'd told Grace she hoped to get into an apartment of her own by the first of the year. And she was planning to sign up for some classes at a nearby community college, with the idea she might become a lab technician.

Anything to get me into a daytime job that has a future,

she'd written. *Mona has been encouraging me; she thinks I'm smart. Can U believe that?*

Grace had smiled sadly when she'd read that last part. Perry was a lot smarter than she'd ever given herself credit for being. Her problem wasn't lack of intelligence. It was lack of self-confidence and lack of self-respect.

Perry had also said she was going to buy Mona's car because Mona planned to get a new one. *They said they'd work out the financing for me.*

Bill and Mona sounded like wonderful people. Grace hoped to meet them one day.

As October drew to an end, Grace was amazed to realize how contented she was. She wasn't making a fraction of what she'd earned at her job in New York, yet she was happy. The work she *was* doing, both in her private practice and at the Sanctuary, was wonderfully satisfying. Maybe it wasn't as challenging, but her clients were so grateful when she helped them and their thanks made her feel useful in ways she'd never felt before.

And Emily was a joy. Grace couldn't imagine a life without her now. Each night as she got the baby ready for bed, then rocked her for a bit before putting her in her crib and kissing her good-night, she sent up a prayer of thanks, both to Perry and to God.

Grace also decided it was time to get a dog. So the last Saturday in October, she put Emily in the car seat and the two of them drove to the animal shelter.

Emily was so excited by the sight of all the animals, she nearly jumped out of her portable stroller.

"Da, da, da," she kept shouting. It was obvious she was trying to say *dog*.

"What a gorgeous child," commented the staff member who was helping them.

Grace beamed as if she were directly responsible for Emily's beauty. "Thank you."

They looked at all the dogs and Grace's heart smote her when she saw the hopeful looks in their eyes. She wished she could take them all, poor things. She settled on a beautiful mixed-breed female puppy that looked as if it had some lab in it. It was a lovely reddish-brown shade and Grace wondered if one of its parents had been a golden retriever.

Emily could hardly contain herself as Grace took care of filling out the forms and writing a check to cover the puppy's shots. Grace was glad she'd brought the stroller, because if she'd had to hold Emily in her arms, she wasn't sure she could have done it. Besides, she wanted to stop by the PetSmart store on the way home and buy a crate, a food and water bowl, dog food and a leash. And maybe some dog toys and treats. She grinned. What the heck. Why not buy a doggy bed, too?

Grace named the puppy Ginger. She knew it wasn't very original, but she didn't care. She liked it, and that's what counted. It was great that the dog—who was three months old—was already trained to do its business outside, because that was one less thing for Grace to worry about.

Ginger would spend her days outdoors. With the covered patio, her crate could stay out there with a nice, soft quilt inside for her to sleep on. Since the yard was fenced, there was no worry of her getting out.

The first night she spent with them, Grace couldn't stop smiling. Ginger and Emily got along like a house afire, and Grace—watching as the dog frolicked and Emily crawled after her—thought that everything in her life had finally fallen into place. The only thing left to do now was to make Emily legally hers.

Perry was now the proud owner of an eight-year-old Honda Civic. She was so thrilled to have her own car, she was almost afraid to drive it.

What if she had a wreck or something? She couldn't stand the idea of putting even the smallest ding on its shiny red surface. Mona had taken such good care of the car, it looked newer than it was. Even the mileage was fairly low—just a little over seventy thousand miles. And it ran perfectly.

On the first Saturday of November, Perry finally decided to drive the car to work. Normally, she just rode in with Bill or, if he decided to go in earlier, Mona dropped her off. But today she wanted to stop at a toy store Angie had told her about, so she would christen the car.

She arrived at the store safely and spent a pleasurable thirty minutes looking at the stuffed animals. Grace had mentioned that Emily loved stuffed animals, and Perry wanted to send her one. She narrowed her choices down to two and finally decided on an adorable skunk with a tag saying its name was Stinky.

She was grinning as she walked into the bar a half hour later.

"What're you so happy about?" Angie asked.

"I drove my car to work, I bought Emily a stuffed animal and I have a new picture of her that Grace e-mailed me yesterday."

"If we put up any more pictures, people won't even know this place is a bar," Angie said.

Perry laughed. But it was true. Bill had taped pictures of Emily all over the place. One, a gorgeous photo Grace had taken at the beach, he'd had blown up and it occupied a place of honor in the middle of the mirror behind the bar. Perry looked at it now. It was a full face shot and Emily was laughing, her big eyes alight with happiness. She looked so beautiful.

Sometimes Perry wanted to cry, thinking about what she'd given up. But most of the time, she was just happy Grace had Emily and that she was generous and kind and kept Perry updated on what was going on in Emily's life. Perry hadn't told Grace yet, but she was planning to go to Florida for Christmas. Going would push back her plan to move into her own place by the first of the year, but she'd talked it over with Bill and Mona, and they'd encouraged her to go.

"We love having you here with us," Mona had said.

"Anyway, I think it's important you go to see your family. They need to see with their own eyes how well you're doing."

It was a slow afternoon, and Perry was still thinking about the trip to Florida and how nice it would be to see Emily in person when the front door opened and two women walked in.

Perry stared, then froze. She had immediately recognized one of the women. It was Glenda. Glenda, who had introduced her to Johnny, Emily's father.

Ohmigod.

Bill smiled at the women, who laughingly decided to sit on bar stools instead of at one of the tables.

Perry didn't know what to do. Would Glenda recognize *her?*

Bill gave Perry a curious look. She knew he was probably wondering why she didn't walk up to Glenda and her friend, ask them what she could get them. But Perry was paralyzed and couldn't seem to make her feet work.

And then Glenda turned her way. She gave Perry a curious look, then her eyes widened and she grinned. "Perry!" she said. "It *is* you, isn't it?"

So Perry forced her feet to move, and she walked over to where they sat. "Yep, it's me," she said as casually as she could. "Hi, Glenda. Long time no see."

"I know. It's been, what? Two years?"

"Something like that." Turning to Bill, she said, "Bill, this is an old friend. Glenda and I worked together for a while a couple of years ago."

"Hi, Bill," Glenda said. "And this is my friend, Vicky."

The other woman smiled and said hi.

"What have you been doing with yourself?" Perry asked.

"I'm living up in L.A. now. Just down here for the weekend, visiting family," Glenda said.

"What can we get you?" Bill asked.

"I'll do it, Bill," Perry said.

"What do you have on draft?" Vicky asked.

Perry told them, and both she and Glenda said they'd take the beer on draft. Perry walked away to fill their order. Just as she turned around, full glasses in hand, Glenda looked up and her gaze fastened on the huge photo of Emily taped to the mirror.

"Whose baby is that?" she asked Bill. She kept staring at the picture.

He grinned proudly. "That's Perry's baby. Isn't she gorgeous?"

"Yours?" Glenda said, turning to look at Perry, who put the glasses of beer in front of her and Vicky. "Really? How old is she?"

Perry tried not to betray the fear that had suddenly struck her. "Um, she's almost eleven months old."

"No kidding." Glenda turned her gaze back to the picture. "So who's the dad? That old boyfriend of yours? What was his name? Dan? Dale?" She drank some of her beer.

Perry's heart was beating too fast. Why was Glenda asking? "Yes," she lied.

"So you two got back together then, huh?"

Perry nodded. "For a while." She wondered what Bill was thinking. She knew he could hear what she and Glenda were talking about. She was grateful Angie was on her break because she knew about Johnny—one of the few people who did.

Glenda took out a pack of Marlboros and lit one. She took a deep drag and blew the smoke out slowly. "So who watches her while you work?"

"My sister has her," Perry said. Desperate to change the subject, she said, "So where are you working in L.A.?"

"At one of the clubs on the Strip."

"Really? Which one?"

But Glenda was once more looking at Emily's picture. "You wouldn't believe how much she looks like my cousin's little girl."

At the word *cousin*, Perry's heart lurched painfully. She began wiping the bar. She didn't look at Glenda.

"They could be twins," Glenda continued thoughtfully. "The only difference is the color of their hair. Lisa's baby's hair is lighter, but man, otherwise they look *exactly* alike."

Because Perry had to say something, she said, "They say everyone has a twin somewhere."

"Yeah," Vicky chimed in. "I'm always meeting people who say I look just like someone they know."

Glenda smiled and nodded.

Perry wished she wouldn't keep staring at Emily's picture. She wished Bill had never put those pictures up. Why had she let him? What had she been *thinking*?

"What's your baby's name?" Glenda asked.

Perry swallowed. "Emily." She didn't dare look at Bill, who had walked down to where the women were seated. *Please, please, please don't say anything.*

"So when did your sister move here?"

Oh, God. There was no help for it. Perry couldn't tell another lie, not with Bill standing right there. "She didn't. She lives in Florida."

"But I thought you said—"

"My sister adopted Emily."

Glenda opened her mouth to ask another question, but just then, in answer to Perry's silent prayer, the door opened and a half dozen noisy sailors walked into the bar. They headed straight for the bar stools, and one of them, a good-looking redhead, started to flirt with Glenda.

Thank you, God, Perry thought. Now both she and Glenda would be too busy to talk. Walking over to the sailors, she took their orders, and she and Bill began to fill them. She purposely waited on the sailor who was farthest from Glenda, and when he began to flirt with her, she flirted back. All the while she was silently praying that Glenda and Vicky would leave.

The two women finally finished their beers and got up about twenty minutes later. The sailors protested, but Glenda and Vicky just laughed and said they had to go, they were meeting Glenda's mother at the mall. Glenda waved at Perry as they walked past. "It was nice seeing you again, Perry. If you're ever up in L.A., look me up."

Perry said she would. She began to breathe easy again after Glenda was gone. She knew it was silly to have gotten so upset. The only reason Glenda had asked so many questions about Emily was because she was nosy. She always had been. Still, the questions worried Perry, even though she figured Glenda would never, not in a million years, connect Emily to Johnny.

But even though she continued to tell herself there was no reason to worry, she wondered if she should tell Grace what had happened. By the time her shift was over—she no longer stayed till closing, but was off at midnight—she had decided telling her would worry Grace needlessly.

Best just to forget the whole thing.

An older sister is a friend and defender, a listener,
conspirator, a counselor and a sharer of delights—
and sorrows, too.

—*Pam Brown*

CHAPTER 20

On Monday, as soon as Grace got to her office, she
picked up the phone and called Craig.

"Grace!" he said. "How nice to hear from you."

"Hello, Craig. How are you?"

"I'm doing fine. Boy, you've really made a splash in
Seacrest, haven't you? I've been seeing your name everywhere."

"You read that story about me in the paper, didn't you?"

"Yep. It was a nice one."

"It's brought me quite a bit of business."

"Good. I'm glad."

"Even though we're competitors?"

"There's plenty of room here for more than one legal
eagle."

Grace smiled. "In New York they called me a shark."

"In Miami they called *me* a shyster."

"I don't believe that."

"I'm only kidding." His voice softened. "I've missed you, Grace."

Grace didn't know what to say. She didn't want to lie, yet she also didn't want to hurt his feelings, because basically, Craig was a pretty nice guy.

He seemed to understand how she felt. "You don't have to say anything. I just wanted you to know how I feel."

"Thank you." She cleared her throat. "The reason I called is, I'm ready to go forward with Emily's adoption."

"Were you able to talk with your sister regarding Emily's father?"

"Yes, but she doesn't know anything more than she's already told me."

"So she couldn't give you any additional information?"

"No."

"Which means it'll be virtually impossible to track him down."

It was obvious to Grace he was thinking aloud. "I don't see how we could."

"And your sister reiterated that she never told him she was pregnant."

"He was long gone when she found out."

"And she doesn't know how to get in touch with that cousin of his."

"No. She's not even sure of her last name. Or where she's living now."

"Okay, then. I'll have the petition to adopt drawn up, and we'll go from there."

"Great. After the filing, how long will the adoption take?"

"Since you're related to Emily by blood, it may not take long at all. The judge has the authority to waive the waiting period and finalize the adoption within weeks."

"So Emily can be mine by Christmas?" Grace said. What a wonderful Christmas present *that* would be.

"Easily, I'd say."

After they'd said goodbye, Grace felt so giddy, she knew she'd never be able to get anything constructive done that day, so she decided to close up shop, collect Emily from the day-care center, and spend one last lovely day on the beach before Seacrest's version of winter set in.

Maybe they'd even stop by the house and get Ginger and take her with them.

Grace practically skipped to her car. If she were any happier, she was afraid she'd burst.

The adoption proceedings turned out to be a formality. The judge—one of the lenient ones, Craig said—looked at the adoption petition, the copy of Emily's birth certificate, the notarized document Perry had signed giving up her parental rights and stating that she wanted Grace to have Emily and all Grace's financial records.

After that, Meg testified on Grace's behalf as did her mother and her aunt.

"I see no reason why this adoption can't be finalized immediately," Judge Richards said.

Grace forced herself not to leap up, run to the bench and throw her arms around the judge. Instead, she just beamed at Craig.

An hour later, she was the proud bearer of a new birth certificate for Emily, one that listed Grace as her mother. Tears filled her eyes as she hugged her mother and aunt, and then Meg. She even hugged Craig.

"I'm happy for you, Grace," he said.

Grace was so grateful and happy herself, she invited him to come to the celebration dinner she had just decided to hold that evening at Piccolo's, the restaurant she had been introduced to by him.

So that evening, Grace and Emily, Meg, Craig, Stella and Mutt gathered at the restaurant. They were seated at a round corner table by the windows and, as they watched the sun setting over the sparkling Gulf, Grace's aunt raised her wineglass.

"To Grace and Emily," she said, "and the new family they formed today. May your futures be filled with all of life's blessings."

Grace knew she was going to cry. But that was okay. Today was a day it was all right to be emotional. Because today she had become a mother.

For days after leaving San Diego, Glenda thought about Perry Campisi's baby and how much she looked like her cousin Lisa's little girl. Perry had said the baby was almost eleven months old, which meant she'd probably been born in early January. Glenda counted backward. So Perry had gotten pregnant sometime in early April. Glenda thought about it some more, then she went to her storage closet and pulled out the box where she kept her old diaries. She'd started keeping a yearly diary since she'd received one as a birthday present when she'd turned thirteen.

Last year's diary was on the top. She flipped through the pages, turning to the month of March, and started reading the entries.

There it was! March 22nd.

Perry and Cookie and I went to a party one of Johnny's buddies was giving at a bar near the base. Man, did we ever get wasted. But we had a great time. And Perry and Johnny sure hit it off. They were all over each other.

The next day's entry read:

Talked to Johnny today and tried to warn him not to fall for Perry because she's on the rebound right now—Don's been jerking her around—but he just laughed at me. I'm just having fun, he said. She's hot stuff.

Glenda remembered how Johnny and Perry had been together for the next two weeks. Soon after, Johnny had shipped out. And a week or two later, Perry's boyfriend had come back.

Maybe Perry had told her the truth. Maybe Don really was the baby's father.

But Glenda couldn't get past how much her baby looked like Lisa's baby. And, by extension, how much she looked like Lisa and Johnny. Because Lisa and Johnny were twins. They both had those unusual blue eyes and deep dimples. Glenda used to be so envious of those dimples. When they were all in the sixth grade, she used to walk around with her finger pushed into her cheek, hoping *she'd* get dimples, too.

Thoughtfully, Glenda stowed the diary away. Then she walked into the kitchen where her cell phone was charging. Picking it up, she scrolled through the saved numbers and pressed the one labeled Lisa.

Ten minutes later, she had Johnny's new phone number written on a piece of paper. And five minutes after that, he was saying, "Hello?"

"Hey, Johnny, it's Glenda. How you doing? Married life treating you okay?"

"Glenda!" he said happily. "Hey, it's good to hear from you. Married life is great."

Johnny was just back from his honeymoon. He'd married an old high-school girlfriend, someone he'd reconnected with at their class reunion five months earlier.

"How's L.A.?" he said.

"L.A.'s fine. Hey, Johnny, something weird happened a week or so ago, and I wanted to tell you about it. But first, is DeeDee there?"

"Nah, she went to get her hair cut."

"Okay, good." So Glenda told him about going to San

Diego and how she and Vicky had gone to Digger's and how she'd run into Perry. "You remember Perry Campisi, don't you?"

"Oh, yeah," he said, laughing. "That girl was crazy. We had some good times together."

"Well, this is the strange thing." Then she told him about the baby pictures and how she'd been struck by the eerie resemblance between Perry's baby and Lisa's baby. "The thing is, Johnny, that baby is the spitting image of you. She's got Perry's black hair, but other than that, she's you all over again. And," she added, "I figured out from what Perry said that she got pregnant at the end of March or early April." She let that sink in.

"Damn," he said after a while. "So you think…?"

"Yeah, I think…"

"Holy shit."

"She hasn't got the baby, though. She said her sister adopted her and they live in Florida."

"Jeez, Glenda, you sure know how to drop a bombshell, don't you?"

"I'm sorry. But I thought you should know."

"Yeah. I—I'll have to think about this."

"Yeah, I figured you would."

"Is that the sister that's the lawyer?"

"Perry told you about her, huh?"

"Only that she had one sister who was a lawyer in New York. That was about *all* she told me. As you know, we didn't spend much time talking."

"The sister's name is Grace. I remember that because I love that name. I remember thinking how if Mom was gonna give me a name starting with G, why couldn't it have been Grace instead of Glenda?" She laughed. "She's not married, either. At least she wasn't two years ago. Perry told me the sister is one of those who always got straight As. Guess she was the perfect one and Perry was the wild one."

"Jesus, Glenda, what do you think I should do?"

"Depends. Do you care?"

"Hell, yes, I care. I mean, if it's my kid…"

"Yeah, I thought you'd say that." Johnny had always been a sucker for kids. One time when they'd all been talking, he and Lisa and Glenda and her brother Tom, Johnny had said he'd like to have at least six kids. She remembered how they'd teased him, but he hadn't backed down. "You gonna tell DeeDee?"

"Guess I'll have to if I decide to do anything about it."

"Well, I just thought you should know. Call me if you want to talk about it again, okay?"

"Yeah, I will."

After they'd hung up, Glenda sat there and stared into space. Maybe she should have just minded her own business. But if Johnny had a baby, didn't he have the right to know? Well, it was too late to change anything now. She'd told Johnny and from here on, things were out of her hands.

Grace had never cooked Thanksgiving dinner before, but this year she decided to try. She invited Meg, her mother and her aunt to come, warning them first that the food might not be edible.

"Knowing your penchant for perfection," Meg said, "I find that hard to believe. What can I bring?"

"How about some dessert?"

"Okay. I make a mean key lime pie. Or would you rather have pumpkin?"

"I'd rather have the key lime, but my mother's a traditionalist."

"Tell you what, I'll bring both."

Grace groaned. "I'm not sure my waistline can stand it."

"Good grief, Grace, if you were any thinner, we wouldn't be able to see you."

"The woman exaggerates shamelessly," Grace said to Emily, who was playing with Ginger on the floor by Grace's feet while she talked on the phone.

Emily laughed, pulling at Ginger's ear, and Ginger barked.

"Stop that, Emily," Grace said. "It's not nice to pull Ginger's ears."

Emily gave her a dark look. Grace stifled a smile. Her daughter was quickly developing a mind of her own, and she *hated* being corrected. Like mother, like daughter, Grace thought proudly.

"What time do you want me?" Meg was asking.

"Come at one. We'll plan to eat about two."

"Can't wait."

The meal turned out to be wonderful. Grace had

followed her mother's instructions exactly and was surprised at how easy it was to fix the turkey and dressing.

"This is the best dressing I've ever eaten," Meg said, patting her stomach. "But it's really different from what I'm used to."

"That's because this is *northern* dressing," Stella said, "not southern." She grinned. "And we call it stuffing, not dressing. The reason it's so good is, it's made with white bread instead of cornbread. And lots of butter."

"Well, whatever you call it, it's delicious."

"You did do a good job, Grace," her mother said.

Mutt laughed. "Did you think she *wouldn't?* Miss I-Must-Do-Everything-Perfectly?"

They all laughed.

"Oh, stop it, you guys," Grace said.

"Grace, if you're going to live in Florida, you have to learn to say *y'all* instead of *you guys*," Meg said.

Grace rolled her eyes.

Emily, too, enjoyed herself. She ate cranberry sauce, mashed potatoes, peas and stuffing. Grace hoped she didn't get sick from all the rich food.

After dessert, they sat around over second cups of coffee, then Meg said she had to be going. "Tomorrow's a workday for me, you know."

"I'll come in tomorrow for a while," Grace said, "if Mom and Aunt Mutt will watch Emily."

"We'd love to," they said almost in unison.

After Meg had gone, Grace said, "Shall we call Perry?"

They'd already talked to Sal and Jen. Even Michael—
who wasn't the best about remembering to call—had
phoned earlier to wish them a happy Thanksgiving.

Her mother smiled. "Let's."

But there was no answer at the Winterses' home, and
Grace didn't leave a message. "I'll just e-mail her," she said
to her mother, who was visibly disappointed.

Grace wondered where they all were. Perry hadn't said
she was spending Thanksgiving with Bill and Mona, but
Grace had assumed she would. Then again, Perry didn't
tell Grace everything she was doing.

Probably a good thing, Grace thought. Everyone
deserved to have some secrets.

The next morning, when Grace walked into the shelter,
Meg said, "Guess who's back."

"Who?"

"Remember Anna?"

"The one with the three kids and the girl named Lizzie?"

"That's the one."

"What happened this time?"

"Same thing. Her husband lost his temper and hit her.
Knocked out a couple of teeth."

"He must have hit her really hard to do that."

"And the little girl has bruises on her arms. Anna said
he was squeezing her arms because he said she was disre-
spectful."

Grace sighed. "Is she going to press charges this time?"

"I think she might."

"Where is she?"

"Helping to clean up the kitchen. I'll go and get her."

A few minutes later Meg came back with Anna. The woman's eyes were bleak, and she looked thinner than before.

Grace sighed mentally. She hoped Anna would see reason this time. "Hello, Anna," she said gently.

"Hello." The word came out muffled because Anna tried to say it without opening her mouth.

Probably embarrassed about the missing teeth, Grace realized. Sympathy for the woman mixed with exasperation because, dammit, this latest episode need not have happened. If Anna had just left that husband of hers the *first* time she'd shown up at the shelter, it *wouldn't* have happened.

"Meg tells me you are ready to take some action against your husband," Grace said.

Anna turned stricken eyes to Meg.

"Anna, you have to unless you want this kind of thing to happen again. And it *will* happen again," Meg said. "And from my experience, each time it happens, it'll be worse than the time before."

"Until eventually he kills you or one of your children," Grace said. The time for gentleness was past. Now it was time for brutal honesty.

"He would never do that," Anna cried. "He...Jake isn't bad. H-he's just so frustrated right now."

"Most men who kill their wives aren't bad," Grace said. "But they still kill them. Do you want to take that chance?"

Anna shook her head miserably.

"Your husband needs help. And the only way he'll get it is if you force him to," Meg said.

Anna chewed on her bottom lip. Finally she sighed and said, "What will happen to him if I press charges?"

"He'll be arrested and taken to jail."

"Oh, God," Anna said.

Meg put her hand on Anna's arm. "This is for your protection and that of your children. And it's for your husband's own good."

A tear slid down Anna's face. Finally she nodded.

"You need to be prepared," Grace said. "They'll want to take photos of you at the police station—for evidence. It can be a humiliating experience." Grace hated having to tell her because the last thing she wanted was for Anna to change her mind, but it was only fair to warn her. "Will you be okay with that?"

"Y-you'll be with me?"

"Yes," Grace said. "I'll be with you every step of the way."

"Then I can do it."

Later, as Grace left the police department where she had accompanied Anna while she filed charges against her husband, she thought about how glad she was that she'd never been dependent on a man. Of course, most men were not like Anna's Jake, but still... It was best to have options...to be able to support yourself if you needed to. Even if you were married to someone wonderful, what happened if he died? Or was suddenly unable to work?

Look at Perry. She was a perfect example. If she'd been independent and able to earn a decent living, she would have been able to keep Emily and raise her herself.

But if she had, then Grace wouldn't have had Emily, would she? And that didn't bear thinking about.

Sisters are connected throughout their lives by a special bond—whether they try to ignore it or not. For better or for worse, sisters remain sisters, until death do them part.

—Brigid McConville

CHAPTER 21

Grace, who had never cared much for Christmas, now could hardly wait for the holiday. Having Emily was what made the difference. She'd already begun buying toys, and the other day she'd seen the most beautiful burgundy velvet dress with white lace around the collar and sleeves. Emily would look gorgeous in it. Grace might even take her to a professional photographer and have a Christmas picture taken.

She could even have the picture put on greeting cards! She grinned like a nut, thinking how much fun it would be to send cards to all the people she used to work with. Everyone she knew, as a matter of fact. Why not? It was Emily's first Christmas, and Grace's first Christmas as a parent. She deserved to enjoy it.

Today, a Saturday in early December, she and Emily were going shopping for ornaments and other decorative items for the house. For the first time in her adult life, Grace was going to have a Christmas tree, and she intended to make the most of it.

It was a beautiful, balmy Gulf coast day, so different from winter weather in New York. Grace dressed in clogs, comfortable jeans and a short-sleeved sweater and put the baby in soft denim pants and a long-sleeved T-shirt. She had packed up the diaper bag and was just about ready to leave when the doorbell rang.

"Damn," she muttered. Sighing, she walked to the front door and peered out the peephole. A youngish man she didn't recognize stood on the doorstep.

"Who is it?" she called.

"Grace Campisi?" he called back.

"Yes. Who are you? What do you want?"

"My name is John Kimball. I'd like to talk to you."

"What about?"

"Miss Campisi, could you please open the door? I don't want to shout."

"I don't open the door to strangers."

There was a silence. What the *hell* did he want? Even if she *didn't* open the door, she could hardly leave now. He'd see her go into the carport. If he was dangerous, he might accost her.

"I need to talk to you. I think I'm Emily's father."

Grace's heart slammed into her chest. "Wh-what did you say?" she whispered. But of course, he couldn't hear her.

"Miss Campisi?"

Grace swallowed. Her hands were shaking.

"Please open the door so we can talk. You can keep it on the chain," he said.

She didn't have a chain on the door.

"Or we can talk outside," he said.

Grace glanced over at the baby, who was in the playpen happily playing with the stuffed skunk Perry had sent her. No possible harm could come to her with Grace right outside the door. Grace reached over and turned the dead bolt. Then she opened the door and walked out onto the stoop. The man—John Kimball, he'd said— gave her a tentative smile. "I'm sorry to just say it out like that," he said, "but I didn't know how else to make you listen to me."

Grace said the first thing that came to her mind. "H-how did you find me?" She was transfixed by the glimpse of dimples when he'd smiled. And by the distinc-tive slate-blue color of his eyes. Dear God. Emily's eyes. Emily's dimples. Grace's heart was pounding like a trip-hammer, and she felt as if she might faint.

"You can find anybody on the Internet," he said. "I knew about you from your sister, and my cousin Glenda told me your name and that you'd moved to Florida. It only took me twenty minutes to get an address."

"I—I just don't understand." But, of course, she *did*.

Maybe she could bluff him. She wet her lips. "What makes you think you're Emily's father?"

"My cousin saw a picture of Emily. She said she looks just like me."

Grace's mind raced wildly. She was so frightened she wanted to run back into the house, slam the door in his face, take Emily and disappear somewhere where this man would never again find her. "So?" she said coldly. "Lots of people look alike, don't they?"

"The reason I believe I could be Emily's father is that Perry and I were together in late March and early April. That's when Emily had to be conceived, because she was born the first week of January, wasn't she?"

All Grace's years of training as a tough lawyer deserted her. Now she was just another woman frightened out of her wits. She had no idea how his cousin had seen a picture of Emily or how they knew when Emily had been born. When the adoption had been finalized, those birth records had been sealed. Had Perry *seen* the cousin? If so, why hadn't she told Grace?

"None of that matters," she said. "I've adopted Emily legally. Perry signed away her rights. And as far as you're concerned, anyone could say he's Emily's father. That doesn't make it so."

"I realize that. But I'm prepared to go to court and take legal steps to find out the truth."

"But *why?*" Grace cried. "I've *adopted* her. I'm the only

mother she's ever known. What purpose will be served by
going to court?"

Although he looked harmless, with an open, friendly
face, his eyes were steely as they met hers. "If she's really my
daughter, Miss Campisi, I want her. I will file for custody."

"It doesn't matter what you want. The adoption is final."

"I've spoken to a lawyer. He tells me I have an extremely good chance of overturning the adoption."

Grace shook her head. "No! You can't just waltz in here
and…I'll fight you with everything I've got. I'm not giving
her up. I love her, and she loves me. You haven't even *seen*
her. Now go away. I don't want to talk to you anymore."

"I'm sorry to upset you. I know how you must feel—"

"You don't know *anything!* I gave up my job, my apartment, my life in New York. I gave up *everything* for Emily.
She means the world to me. I won't let you take her."

He shrugged. "Well, we'll see, won't we?"

For a long moment, their gazes held, then he turned and
walked to a car that was parked at the curb. Only then did
Grace see the woman in the car. Young, pretty, with straw-
berry-blond hair, she had been watching them.

His girlfriend? Grace wondered. Or was that the
infamous cousin? But Grace didn't really care who she
was. As far as she was concerned, she didn't want to know
anything about John Kimball. She just wanted him to go
away and stay away.

Ten minutes later, the front door once more locked,
Grace picked up her cell phone and called Craig's

number. *Please answer*, she prayed, as the number rang several times. When his voice mail kicked in, she nearly cried.

"Craig, it's Grace. I must talk to you as soon as possible. It's urgent. Please call me on my cell." She gave him the number even though she knew he had it. Then she disconnected the call.

From her vantage point, she could see Emily still happily playing. Ginger was settled next to the playpen, watching her. Every once in a while, Emily would put her fingers through the holes in the webbing, and Ginger would lick them. When she did, Emily would laugh.

Grace's eyes filled with tears.

Oh, God. I can't lose her. I can't.

Christmas shopping was forgotten. Now all she could think about was the horrific surprise she'd gotten this morning. Her mind whirled chaotically. She couldn't seem to get it organized into coherent thought. She had so many questions.

Perry!

She needed to call Perry.

Hurriedly, Grace found the number for the Winterses' home and called it. It rang three times, then a soft female voice said, "Hello?"

"Mrs. Winters?"

"Yes?"

"This is Grace Campisi, Perry's sister. Is Perry there?"

"Oh, hello, Grace. Yes, she's upstairs. I think I heard her

get out of the shower a few minutes ago. Hold on, and I'll
see if she can come to the phone."

Grace heard the woman call Perry and a muffled answer
in reply. "Pick up the extension," the woman called.

A minute later Perry was on the line.

"Oh, thank God," Grace said.

"Grace? What's wrong?" Perry asked.

So Grace told her.

"Oh, no," Perry kept saying.

"How did his cousin see Emily's picture, anyhow?"

Grace's heart sank as Perry told her how Bill had plas-
tered pictures of Emily all over the bar.

"I'm so sorry, Grace. B-but he knows how proud of her
I am, and really, it was a sweet thing to do."

"Why didn't you *call* me?" Grace wanted to scream.
Such an innocent thing, putting up pictures of Emily.
Who would have imagined it would cause her entire world
to be turned upside down?

"I—I thought about it, but I didn't want to worry you,"
Perry said.

"Oh, God," Grace said.

"W-what is Johnny going to do?"

"He says he'll go to court and file for custody."

"Can he do that?"

"Oh, yes, he can do it."

"But...but *you're* her mother. The adoption is final.
You said so yourself."

"Doesn't matter," Grace said. "Remember that case a

few years ago where the birth father hadn't been told about his son's birth and claimed him after that couple had legally had him for something like three or four years? The court overturned *that* adoption. The birth father had rights, and they were violated. Oh, God, I'll never forget how that little boy cried when they took him away from his adoptive parents."

"Oh, Grace, that's terrible! Should...should I come?"

"I don't think you being here would make any difference."

"But why not? I'm Emily's mother."

"You signed away your parental rights. You won't have a say in court."

"Oh, Grace. This is awful. You mean Johnny may *get* Emily? That they may take her *away* from you?"

Tears pooled in Grace's eyes. "Yes," she said brokenly, "that's exactly what I mean."

Craig didn't call until late that afternoon. "I'm sorry, Grace. I was out on the golf course and had my cell turned off."

"It's okay," Grace said tiredly. She had been over and over her options. None of them were good.

Craig listened quietly as Grace brought him up to date on everything that had happened, starting with John Kimball's unexpected visit.

"I won't kid you," he said when she'd finished. "This doesn't sound good."

"Maybe the court won't give any credence to what he says."

"They have to, Grace. Especially given the circumstances. Perry *did* say the father's name was Johnny. And you said yourself, there's a striking resemblance between him and Emily. At the very least, the court will order DNA testing."

"What if I say no?"

"Grace…"

She sighed. "I know. I can't say no. But, Craig, won't they take into account the fact that I've raised Emily practically since she was born? And that Perry wanted me to have her?"

"Grace, you know as well as I do that the father's rights will supercede yours. Especially if, as you say, he's a decent man."

"What am I going to do, Craig?" Grace cried.

"I'm sorry, Grace, but there's nothing much you can do right now. The ball's in his court."

She could run. She could rent a trailer, pack up everything they owned and move to Mexico. The court couldn't touch her in Mexico. Or she could go to Italy. Grace loved Italy. She used to dream of retiring there. And her Italian wasn't bad. But even as she thought it, she knew she wouldn't do it. For one thing, she believed in the law. She'd sworn to uphold the law. For another, she wasn't rich. What would she do for money? Hers would run out within a year. Eventually, she might be able to practice law somewhere else, but first she'd have to learn their laws. It would take years of study. And even if she could bring herself to break the laws of her own country, did she really want to live as a fugitive? Is that the kind of life she wanted for Emily?

"So we just wait?" she finally asked.

"I'm afraid so."

"That stinks."

"I know it does."

"You'll continue to represent me in this, won't you, Craig?"

"You know I will."

After they hung up, Grace thought about calling her mother, but she just couldn't face it. Besides, ignorance *was* bliss. Why not let her mother and aunt be happy as long as they could be?

It was Wednesday before Craig called Grace to say that as the lawyer who'd represented her in the adoption proceedings, he'd been notified by the court that John Kimball was claiming to be Emily's father and had filed a petition asking that her adoption be overturned. Craig said Grace's presence was required in court the following Monday.

With a heavy heart, Grace rescheduled that afternoon's appointments, then closed the office. After picking Emily up at the day-care center, she drove to her mother's.

"Grace!" her mother said when she saw her. "What a nice surprise." But her smile quickly faded when she saw the expression on Grace's face. "What is it?"

"Oh, Mom," Grace said, tearing up. "The most awful thing has happened." And then she started to cry in earnest.

Emily, upset by Grace's tears, started to pat her face. Then her little face crumpled and she started to cry, too.

"Grace, you're scaring me," her mother said. She reached for Emily. "Here, let me take her."

By now Grace's aunt had come into the living room. "Goodness sakes," she said, looking from one to the other. "What's going on?"

"Take the baby, Mutt," Grace's mother said. Then she took Grace's arm and led her to the sofa. "What can I get you, Grace? A glass of water? Tissues? A good stiff drink?"

Grace struggled to get herself under control. "Just tissues," she said.

Her aunt put Emily in the playpen that now occupied a corner of the living room. The baby was soon playing with a set of brightly colored plastic blocks.

"Now," her aunt said, "tell us."

Once again Grace repeated the story of the events that had taken place Saturday morning.

Her mother covered her mouth halfway through the story. Her green eyes were stricken. Mutt looked appalled.

"H-He can't really do this, can he, Grace?" her mother asked when she'd finished.

Mutt reached out and clasped Stella's hand.

Grace sighed heavily. "I'm afraid he can."

"But—" Stella began. Then she sank back into her chair. She looked over at Emily, who was banging one block against another. Her eyes filled with tears.

For a long moment, no one spoke.

Then Mutt said quietly, "We mustn't give up hope. We must pray and think positive and pray some more."

"What if Perry comes and says *she* wants Emily?" Grace's mother said suddenly. "Wouldn't *that* make a difference? Doesn't the court always favor the mother?"

"Mom, Perry signed away her rights," Grace said.

"But if she's changed her mind…"

"It won't matter to the court. They won't look favorably on a woman who gave away her baby, who lied on Emily's birth certificate—"

"She didn't lie!" Stella protested. "She didn't know his last name. What was she supposed to do? Just put down *Johnny?*"

"They'll consider it lying, because technically, the father *wasn't* unknown to her."

"But if she had no idea where to find him…"

"Mom, believe me, I've thought about all this and talked to Craig about it and in the last two days, I've practically *lived* on the Internet studying case law and researching adoption law for any loophole or precedent I could find. And *everything* is in John Kimball's favor."

Perry knew Grace must hate her now.

If only there was something she could do. She thought about going to Florida, anyway, even though Grace had told her not to. But then she thought about what the judge might say and what she would do if he were to ask her, point blank, if Johnny was Emily's father. She'd be under oath; she'd have to tell the truth. It had been dif-

ferent when she'd told the hospital personnel that Emily's
father was unknown. He really *was* unknown then because
she hadn't known his last name or how to contact him.

But everything was different now.

*I've really made a mess of things this time. And now Grace
and Emily are going to pay the price.*

Disconsolate, Perry cried herself to sleep.

Flanked by her mother and her aunt, Grace arrived at
the family court building on the dot of nine. Craig was
waiting for them outside. "We've drawn Judge Richards
again," he said to her.

"Is that good?"

He nodded. "It's the best we could hope for."

When their party walked into the courtroom, Grace saw
that John Kimball and the woman she'd seen in his car were
already there with a woman she assumed to be his lawyer.

"Yes," Craig said to her question. "That's Sue Aldrich.
She's a damn fine lawyer."

John Kimball turned to look at Grace. He whispered
something to the young woman beside him.

Grace looked away. Her heart was beating too fast, and
she took several deep breaths to calm herself. She and
Craig took their seats at the table on the right side of room.

A moment later, the bailiff said, "All rise," and Judge
Richards came into the courtroom.

The judge sat, then listened gravely as Sue Aldrich
stood and presented the Kimball petition.

When Grace heard the lawyer say "John Kimball and his wife, Dorothy," her heart plummeted. The woman was his wife. He was married. That would make his case even stronger.

"Your Honor," Sue Aldrich said after reading the petition, "Mr. Kimball was recently discharged from the navy and has accepted a position with a large hospital in the San Diego area. He and his wife, Dorothy, although newly married, have already purchased a home. They have a wide network of family support. Mrs. Kimball's family lives only a few miles from their home, and Mr. Kimball's parents and twin sister also live close by. They can provide a loving and stable environment for his daughter."

"Objection," Craig said. "We have yet to establish that Emily Campisi *is* his daughter."

"I agree," the judge said. "And as far as the law's concerned, that's the most important thing we have to know before we can continue. So before hearing any more arguments, I'm ordering DNA testing on both John Kimball and the minor child Emily Campisi. When the results of the tests are known, I'll see everyone back in court." She looked at Sue Aldrich. "Ms. Aldrich, please make the necessary arrangements for your client to be tested and coordinate with Mr. Mancuso about the testing of the child. The bailiff will give you the information about which labs are certified with the county. Your client will pay all costs for both his and the child's tests."

"Thank you, Your Honor," Sue Aldrich said.

Grace looked at Craig. She had never felt so helpless.
Or so frightened.

She was accustomed to *doing* something, taking some
action, when faced with a problem. But in this instance
there was nothing she *could* do.

Except wait.

And pray.

A sister is a gift to the heart, a friend to the spirit, a golden thread to the meaning of life.

—Isadora James

CHAPTER 22

The ten days they had to wait for the results of the DNA tests were the ten longest days of Grace's life.

Grace didn't have to hear the judge say that the DNA tests had proved conclusively that John Kimball was Emily's father. She'd known that was what they'd say ever since she'd seen his eyes and the shape of his face and his dimples.

Still she prayed that Judge Richards would rule in her favor, even as she prepared herself for the worst.

"There are some questions I'd like to ask the parties concerned," the judge said, "before I rule. Does anyone object?"

"No, Your Honor," Sue Aldrich said.

"No, Your Honor," Craig said.

"Mrs. Kimball," the judge said. "How do you feel about raising your husband's child?"

John Kimball's wife smiled. "I'm excited about the possibility, Your Honor. I come from a big family, and I love kids.

In fact, God willing, Johnny and I are hoping to have several more so that Emily will grow up with brothers and sisters."

"And it doesn't bother you to take Emily away from the only mother she's ever known?"

Dorothy Kimball looked over at Grace. "It bothers me a lot, Your Honor. I feel so bad for Miss Campisi, but Emily is Johnny's little girl. He deserves to have her."

"If I overturn the adoption and give Emily to you and your husband, would you be agreeable to Miss Campisi having visitation rights?"

"I, um, don't know, Your Honor." She looked at her husband. "Johnny?"

"It would be okay with me if she wanted to visit Emily," John Kimball said. "She's family, and she loves Emily. What decent person would object to that?"

From the direction of the judge's questions, Grace knew what the outcome of this hearing was going to be. And she was trying to hold herself together. Trying to keep from jumping up and running out of the courtroom. Trying to tell herself that she was strong. That she could survive anything, even this worst of all possible things.

The judge nodded and thanked Dorothy Kimball, then turned to Grace. "Miss Campisi," she said, "this is an unfortunate turn of events. I can only imagine how you must feel, and I wish there were some way I could make everyone happy, but that's not possible. I am truly sorry, but John Kimball was never told he had a child, so in approving your adoption of Emily, his rights were violated. As he is an upstanding citizen and decent young man, I have no choice but to grant his petition to have the adoption overturned and to give him full parental custody of Emily."

It took every bit of Grace's strength not to break down, even though the judge's words were like battering rams against her heart.

Craig reached for Grace's hand under the table. He squeezed it hard.

"Today is Thursday," the judge said, her voice and eyes kind. "You may have until Sunday at noon to turn Emily over to the Kimballs." Addressing her remarks to the Kimballs again, she said, "I'm not going to mandate visitation for Miss Campisi and the child's maternal grandmother, but I hope you will permit it. I'll leave you to work that out between you. Is that satisfactory, Mr. Kimball?"

"Yes, Your Honor," John Kimball said.

The judge nodded. "Also, a new birth certificate will be issued in the name of…" She looked down at her notes. "Emily Grace Kimball, unless you choose to give your child a different name?"

He looked at Grace, then shook his head. "No, Your Honor."

"All right, then," the judge said. "Your attorney may pick up the new birth certificate tomorrow."

Grace was thankful she hadn't allowed her mother and aunt to come to court today. It was hard enough to hold herself together. If she'd had to contend with the two women's heartbreak, she didn't think she could have managed. Blindly, trying not to think, she got up and, led by Craig who held her arm firmly, she headed toward the exit.

"Miss Campisi...Grace, wait!"

Grace turned. John Kimball walked rapidly toward her. "Can we talk for a minute?" he said.

She shook her head. "Not now. I—" She swallowed. "I can't." Her eyes filled with tears, and it was only by force of will that she managed to keep them from overflowing. "T-tomorrow."

"Okay," he said gently. "I understand."

Concentrating only on putting one foot in the front of the other, Grace escaped the courtroom. Outside, Craig walked her to her car.

"I'm so sorry, Grace."

Nodding, she dug in her purse for a tissue, then wiped her eyes and blew her nose.

"We can appeal," he said.

"I know." Damn. She was a regular waterworks. She couldn't seem to stop crying. "But what good would it do? The longer I keep her, the harder it will be to give her up. And I have to think of her." She mopped at her eyes again. "Th-the past week has been hard, and not just for me and my mother. Emily's sensed that something's wrong, and she's been fussy. Not like herself at all." Her agonized eyes met his and saw understanding and compassion. "I have to go now, Craig, before I come completely unglued. Th-thank you for everything."

Leaning forward, he kissed her cheek. "Will you be okay to drive?"

She nodded.

"Be careful. Call me if you want to talk."

"I will."

As she drove away, she saw him standing where she'd left him. She knew he wished he could do something to make things better. But he couldn't fix what was wrong with her. No one could. Her heart had been smashed into millions of pieces, and it would never be whole again.

Grace drove straight to her office where she put a sign on the door saying she would be closed until Monday.

Then, although she wanted to spend every possible minute with Emily, she headed for her mother's. She knew her mother and aunt were anxiously waiting to hear from her, and she didn't want to give them the bad news in Emily's presence. All three of them were going to have to do their crying where Emily couldn't see or hear them.

When she arrived at the apartment, she knocked before letting herself in. When she entered the living room, her mouth dropped open to see Perry standing there.

"You're not mad, are you, Grace? I—I got here early this morning, on the red eye. Mom bought me a ticket."

"No, of course, I'm not mad. I—I'm just surprised."

At her words, Perry rushed forward and threw her arms around Grace.

Grace held her tight. Love constricted her throat. "I'm

so glad you're here." *I should have been the one to send her a ticket. Why didn't I?*

"Oh, Grace, I'm so sorry about everything."

"I know. Me, too." *Please, God, give me the strength to get through this....*

"Grace!" their mother said, entering the living room from the direction of the bedrooms. Grace's aunt Mutt was close behind her. "We heard you come in. What happened? Where's Emily?" The questions came from both of them.

Grace released Perry. She took a deep breath. *Courage.* "We lost," she said gently, trying not to cry again. "The judge overturned the adoption. I—I have to have Emily ready to give to her father on Sunday."

"No!" her mother said, bursting into tears. Then her aunt started to cry, and in seconds, all four women were weeping.

When they'd calmed down a bit, Grace quietly explained what the judge had said.

"I can't believe this," her mother said. "I just can't believe it. W-will we ever *see* her again?"

Grace bit her lip. "I—I don't know. The judge said she hoped her father would allow us to visit. We're supposed to talk tomorrow." Her eyes met Perry's.

"Me, too?" Perry asked.

"I don't know. You weren't mentioned."

Perry bowed her head.

Grace didn't know what to say. She knew her sister was hurting, but right now she was hurting so much herself, she had very little to give anyone else.

For a while, they all fell silent, each lost in her thoughts. Then Grace took a deep, shuddering breath and blew her nose. Standing, she said, "I'm going to go pick up Emily now. I'll bring her back here."

"C-can I come with you, Grace?"

Grace's first reaction was to say no, *she* was Emily's mother, and she wanted and needed to do this herself. But one look at the sorrow in her sister's eyes and the naked longing on her face and Grace couldn't refuse her. She nodded, and Perry gave her a watery smile of thanks.

The rest of the day was easier than Grace would have imagined. Somehow, having Emily with them made the difference. And, in some inexplicable way, Perry's presence helped, too. Emily was fascinated with her new "aunt," and laughed when Perry made faces at her or blew her a raspberry.

Watching them, Grace was oddly comforted. She couldn't have explained why; she only knew the sight of her daughter and her sister together helped to ease the pain in her heart.

That night Grace's aunt Mutt fixed a simple dinner of macaroni and cheese, applesauce and salad. They didn't talk much, they just played with the baby until her eyes began to droop and Grace said it was time for her to take Emily home.

"Come over tomorrow," she told them. "We'll spend the day at my house."

Throughout Friday and Saturday, they were determinedly cheerful, and Grace knew her mother and aunt and sister were doing what she was doing—pushing thoughts of Sunday out of their minds.

Yet it was there, like a ghost in the shadows. Every so often, the ghost would move, and Grace would shiver, knowing that each tick of the clock was bringing the moment of reckoning closer.

As Saturday drew to a close and her mother, her aunt and Perry began to make preparations to go home, Grace hoped they wouldn't ask if they could come to say goodbye in the morning. She knew it was selfish, but she wanted one last morning alone with Emily.

But they didn't ask. Instead, first her mother, then her aunt and finally Perry hugged her tightly. When Perry whispered, "Be strong, Grace," Grace's eyes filled with tears. She was glad Emily was already in bed asleep because she knew when the door closed behind her family, she was going to cry until there were no more tears left.

Giving Emily to the Kimballs was the hardest thing Grace had ever had to do. Saying a final goodbye and putting Emily into John Kimball's arms hurt so much, she could hardly breathe. Dorothy—who was called DeeDee by her husband—clasped Grace's hand and said she would send pictures and whenever Grace wanted to visit, all she had to do was call.

But no matter how kind they were, Grace knew nothing would ever be the same. Emily was going to California. She would be their daughter now, and the memory of Grace would fade quickly. When and if Grace *did* visit, Emily would look upon her as an aunt, someone who sent her cards and presents but didn't figure prominently in her life.

Emily didn't cry until John buckled her into the car seat and she realized Grace wasn't coming with them. Then she began to wail and hold out her arms to Grace. Grace bit her bottom lip hard and willed her eyes to stay dry. "It's okay, sweetheart," she said, leaning into the car. "Here's Stinky. He's going for a ride, too."

Emily's cries abruptly stopped as she saw her favorite toy. Grabbing the stuffed skunk, she hugged it fiercely to her chest and smiled up at Grace. "Mine," she said. *Mine* was her favorite word, one of the first she'd ever learned.

Grace tried to smile back, tried to make herself look cheerful as she backed away from the car.

When the rental car pulled away, Grace stood there stoically, watching until it and its precious occupant were out of sight.

Then she slowly turned and walked into the house she'd bought with so much hope for the future and closed the door behind her. Ginger, who had been sitting there waiting for her return, wagged her tail. Grace knelt and buried her face in the dog's fur.

She'd been wrong last night.

There *were* some tears left.

Having a sister is like having a best friend you can't get rid of. You know whatever you do, they'll still be there.
—*Amy Li*

CHAPTER 23

Grace drifted numbly through the next two weeks. To avoid thinking, she kept herself busy. She packed up the rest of Emily's belongings and took them to UPS to be shipped to the Kimballs. The baby furniture and equipment was taken to the shelter, and Grace turned Emily's room into a home office. Every evening, she stayed at her office late, and when she came home, she cleaned obsessively.

When Ginger, who missed Emily, wandered around the house looking for her with a bewildered expression on her face, Grace tried not to see.

She also tried not to think about the holidays. She knew they would be torture for her. She didn't bother buying a tree. There was no reason to now. *Why?* she thought during the times she could no longer keep her mind blank. *Why did this have to happen? Why did God let me fall in love with Emily, then snatch her away?*

She couldn't help thinking about the only other time she had fallen in love, and how she'd felt when she'd lost Brett. But that was nothing compared to how she felt now. Losing Emily was like having her heart ripped out of her chest.

She didn't cry. Her tears had finally dried up. Crying was a useless activity, anyway. What good did it do? Would it bring Emily back? Would it change anything in Grace's life? Would it make her heart whole again?

She thought about Perry, who had gone back to California. "I had been planning to come to Florida for Christmas," Perry said tearfully when they'd said goodbye. "But now I don't think I will."

Grace had nodded her understanding. She'd hugged Perry hard. She knew her sister was as crushed as she was. In some ways, she wished she could hate Perry. It would make things so much easier if she had a fall guy upon whom to take out her grief and loss. But how could she? Perry had made mistakes, yes, but she had paid for them. And she loved Emily, too. Besides, Grace thought sadly, Perry was her sister. She could never hate her. They were part of each other and always would be.

Grace wondered if Perry would get to see Emily at all. The Kimballs hadn't been receptive to the idea when Grace had broached it.

"She gave her away," John Kimball had said, his voice cold. "I think it'll just be confusing for Emily if Perry tries to be included in her life."

"But you don't object to me or my mother coming out to see her," Grace had said.

"That's different. You're her aunt and her grandmother. Perry's the mother who didn't want her."

"It wasn't that she didn't want her," Grace had tried to explain.

But John Kimball hadn't been in the mood to be forgiving. And really, who could blame him? Perry had not tried to find him. She had lied on Emily's birth certificate. And she had walked away from her baby. None of these things had endeared her to him or would help her case. Grace would just have to hope that in the future he would change his mind.

Grace found herself avoiding spending time with her mother and aunt. It was just too hard looking at their sad faces, and she figured they probably felt the same way about hers. So she stayed away as much as possible.

She also avoided Craig. He'd called several times "just to check up on you," he'd said, and the last time he'd called, he'd asked her if he could take her to dinner.

"It would be good for you to get out, Grace."

She knew his divorce was final, but she just didn't care. "I'm sorry," she'd said. She wasn't sure she'd ever care about anything again.

"I'm sorry, too," he'd said. Then he'd added, "But I'll keep trying. Maybe you'll change your mind one of these days."

Meg tried to get her out of the house, too. "Come on, Grace," she said a few days before Christmas. "Let's go see

a movie. Or better yet, let's hit Jerry's and tie one on."
Jerry's was a local piano bar that Meg liked.

"Thanks, Meg. But I'm not in the mood."

Grace seriously considered putting her house on the
market and moving back to New York. There were just too
many sad memories in Florida. She even went so far as to
e-mail Wallace Finn to feel him out about her returning
to the firm. She got one of those auto-replies saying he was
out of the office until January 2nd.

She didn't put up a tree. And she packed away the ornaments she'd purchased. Maybe she'd use them sometime
in the future. Or maybe she'd just give them away, too.

On Christmas eve, Grace would have stayed home,
but her aunt insisted she come to them. "Please, Grace.
We need you."

I have nothing to give you, Grace wanted to say. Instead
she sighed and said, "All right. But I'm not going to
church." God didn't listen to her prayers and she didn't
blame Him. Why should He? What had she ever done to
deserve His help?

"We'll go to early Mass," her aunt said, "and be back by
seven."

"I'll see you then."

Without enthusiasm, Grace forced herself to go
shopping Christmas eve day. She bought her mother a
pale blue cashmere cardigan sweater and a Coach
handbag. For her aunt, she chose a bottle of L'Air du
Temps perfume and a box of See's milk-chocolate butter

creams, which Grace knew were her favorite. And as she passed the jewelry counter on her way out of the store, she saw a display of Fossil watches and remembered how Meg was always complaining about her watch no longer keeping good time. Impulsively, she chose one of the nicest ones and had it gift wrapped.

Instead of going straight to her mother's, she stopped by the house to pick up a bottle of wine and to make sure Ginger was okay and had enough food and water. Then she headed to the apartment. Her mother and aunt had just gotten back from church when she arrived.

"Hello, honey," her mother said, kissing Grace's cheek.

"Hi, Mom." Grace could see her mother had been crying. Her eyes were puffy.

"I won't say merry Christmas," her aunt said, hugging Grace. "But I will say I love you."

Grace swallowed against the sudden lump in her throat. "I love you, too," she whispered.

Somehow the three of them made it through the evening. Grace's mother had put a ham in the oven before leaving for church, and they ate that and coleslaw and the scalloped-potato casserole her aunt had fixed earlier in the day. Grace wasn't really hungry. She hadn't been hungry since the day John Kimball had shown up on her doorstep. She forced herself to eat, though, because she couldn't afford to lose any more weight. As it was, her clothes were hanging on her. *Pretty soon I'll be a sexless stick.*

Who cared, though?

Who cared about anything?

After dinner, they called Sal and Jen and talked to them and the kids. It was hard, especially when Sal said, "I've been thinking about you, Grace. I'm so sorry about what's happened."

Then they called Michael and Deanna. Perry they would talk to tomorrow.

When the calls were over, they opened their gifts. Grace's mother said she loved the sweater and purse. Her aunt said she loved the perfume and chocolates. And Grace said she loved the Swarovski earrings and bracelet and the red-and-black geometric print silk jacket they'd given her.

But there was no real joy in any of it—the calls to her brothers, the dinner, the gifts, the evening. They were all thinking about the little person who wasn't there. The beautiful child who would never be there again.

At ten o'clock Grace said good-night. But not before her mother insisted that she must come back tomorrow and have dinner with them. "Bring Ginger with you," she said. "I feel sorry for the dog being alone all the time."

The next morning, Grace woke up with a killer headache and a sore throat. It didn't surprise her that she was coming down with something. Whenever she was stressed about something, she got sick. A hot shower and some Advil helped, as did two cups of strong coffee.

She decided she would stop by the shelter to give Meg her gift before going on to her mother's. Ginger was excited to be going somewhere and barked happily as Grace nudged her onto the back seat. Her happiness made Grace feel guilty. Even though *she* was miserable, that was no excuse for neglecting the dog.

"I'm sorry, old girl," she said. "I'll try to do better by you."

As she drove the few blocks from her home to the Sanctuary, she debated whether to tell Meg what she'd decided. If Wallace Finn replied favorably to her e-mail about coming back to work at the firm, she was going to return to New York as soon as she could sell her house. She knew Meg would be disappointed, but Grace felt her friend would understand.

It was noon when Grace arrived at the shelter. She parked in the lot at the side of the building, making sure the windows were cracked for Ginger.

"I'll only be a few minutes," she told the dog, who barked in reply.

She picked up Meg's gift and got out of the car. She had only walked a few steps when she saw a big, dark-haired man approaching. Oh, no. It was Jake Savitch, Anna's husband, the man she'd helped to arrest. She knew he'd made bail because she'd then helped Anna to get a restraining order against him. *Dammit*, she thought. *I don't need this today.*

She wasn't afraid until she saw the gun in his hand. Then she froze and, in a panic, tried to think what to do.

He was obviously distraught. His dark eyes were bleak, his face filled with despair. Quietly, in a voice that scared Grace even more than shouting would have, he said, "You. You're the bitch who ruined my life." His hand shook.

Grace stared at the gun. Her heart was pounding madly.

"I can't even see my own kids on Christmas," he said. "You've turned them all against me. You took my family away from me, so now I'm going to take something away from you."

"You…you don't want to do this," she said as calmly as she could. "If you…hurt me, you'll go back to jail and then what will your family do?"

But he was beyond reasoning. "Say your prayers," he said, just as if she hadn't spoken. He raised the gun.

And as he did, Ginger began to bark.

He jumped, distracted by the barking, and Grace did the only thing she could do. She swung at him with her heavy shoulder bag, trying to knock the gun away from him so she could run. Instead, the gun went off, and Grace felt a hard jolt in her left shoulder.

"Oh," she said, shocked. She looked down at the blood that was already staining her white sweater. There was a buzzing in her head, then she slowly sank to the ground.

Jake Savitch stared at her for a moment, then, uttering something unintelligible, he dropped the gun and ran away.

The buzzing in Grace's head got stronger, and she knew she was going to pass out. Ginger was barking frantically now. Grace tried to find her cell phone in her purse to call 911 but her fingers wouldn't seem to move.

Her last thought before she lost consciousness was of Emily.

Meg heard a dog barking as she pulled into the parking lot. "What in the world?" she said. And then she saw someone lying on the asphalt. "Oh, my God," she said as she got closer and realized it was Grace.

She slammed on the brakes and jumped out of her car. Rushing over to where Grace lay, she quickly realized what must have happened. Whipping out her cell phone, she called 911. Then, while she waited, she pressed her hand against Grace's wound to try to staunch the flow of blood.

"Hang on, Grace," she said, "hang on."

Within minutes, she heard the siren. Then the ambulance was careening into the lot and three EMTs jumped out. Meg, now joined by several staff members and residents of the shelter who'd heard the commotion, stood by helplessly as they worked on Grace, then loaded her into the ambulance.

"Do you want to ride with her?" one of them asked Meg.

"I'll follow you," she said. "I've got to take care of her dog first." She had belatedly realized she couldn't just leave Ginger there. Thank goodness she had Grace's purse because Grace had locked her car. Rushing back to the car, she saw a box on the ground. It was obviously a Christmas present because it was gift-wrapped. When she picked it up, she saw the tag.

To Meg from Grace.

Oh, God. That's why she was here. She was bringing me a present....

Stuffing the box into her purse, Meg unlocked the doors to Grace's car and grabbed Ginger's leash. Then she gave the dog to one of the staff to look after and said she'd be back for Ginger after she made sure Grace was okay.

As she raced toward the hospital, she prayed.

Grace was dreaming. It was a nice dream. She and Emily and Ginger were at the beach, and she didn't want to wake up. But someone was talking nearby, and she knew she had to open her eyes so she could see who it was and tell them to go away and leave her alone.

"She's awake!"

Meg?

What was Meg doing in her bedroom? But this wasn't her bedroom. Her bedroom didn't look like this. It was only then that memory flooded her, and Grace remembered the gun and Jake Savitch and being shot.

"Wh-where am I?" she said through a mouth that felt like cotton.

"You're in the hospital, honey. You were shot. Do you remember that?"

"Mom?"

Sure enough, there was her mother. And her aunt standing behind her. And Meg, too. A moment later, a pleasant-looking nurse shooed them away. "Let me just check her vitals," the nurse said.

When the nurse finished, everyone gathered around her again. "Do you remember what happened?" Meg asked.

"Yes," Grace whispered. "It was Jake Savitch. H-he had a gun."

"I know," Meg said. "He threw it down, I guess, because the police found it after the ambulance took you away."

"Wh-who called the ambulance?"

"I did," Meg said. "I must have pulled into the parking lot only minutes after it happened. Thank God, because even though your injury wasn't life-threatening, you were losing a lot of blood."

"You had to have two blood transfusions," Grace's mother said.

"But you're okay now," her aunt said.

"We were all *so* worried," her mother said.

"Ginger…" Grace said. "She…she was with me."

"Yes," Meg said. "I heard her barking. She's okay, though. I took her home and put her in the backyard."

"And I was bringing you a Christmas present," Grace said.

"I found it," Meg said, smiling. "In fact, I have it here with me."

They talked awhile longer, then Grace's eyes began to close.

"We'll go now," her mother said. "They've given you something for pain, and they said it would make you sleep."

"Okay," Grace said. Right then, she didn't really care about anything except going back to sleep.

"We'll come back in the morning," her aunt said.

Grace slept off and on for most of the rest of the day and night. The next morning, though, she was wide awake and, except for the achy pain in her shoulder, feeling a lot better. She even felt like eating some breakfast. Soon after, the doctor who had taken care of her the day before stopped by to check the dressing on her wound.

"You should be able to go home tomorrow or the next day, at the latest," he said.

As he was leaving her room, an attendant came in carrying a large vase of roses in one hand and a huge basket of fruit in the other.

"My goodness," Grace said. "Are those for *me?*"

"If you're Grace Campisi, they are," the girl said with a smile.

The roses turned out to be from Craig, the basket of fruit from her coworkers at the shelter.

And that wasn't the end of the deliveries. Throughout the rest of the day, visitors bearing flowers, plants and candy continued to arrive. Several of the residents in her mother's building dropped in to see her. Another large arrangement of flowers came from Lucinda Fellows. A gorgeous African violet was sent by Coralee Wainwright, who wrote on the card that she would be by to see Grace later that day. And several others of her clients also sent something. Sylvia French, her mother's neighbor, even brought Grace a small Christmas tree. But the most touching gift of all was a basket of handmade get-well cards from the children staying at the shelter.

Grace laughed through her tears when she read the one from a six-year-old boy she particularly liked. It said, Dear Grace I Hope You Don't Die. Another said, Get Well Soon We Need You.

"Did someone tell these kids what to write?" she asked Frances, the volunteer who'd brought them.

"Nope," Frances said. "They decided what to say all by themselves."

Late in the afternoon, Meg came for the second time that day, and with her was Anna Savitch. She sat by Grace's bed and held her hand. "I'm so sorry about Jake," she said. "And he's real sorry, too. He turned himself in to the police, you know."

"I'm glad," Grace said.

"He scared himself, I think. But you, you were wonderful. You showed so much courage. That's how I want to be someday…just as strong and brave as you are."

"How did all these people know about this?" Grace asked Meg later.

"Honey, a shooting in Seacrest is big news. You made the afternoon edition on Channel 3 yesterday."

Grace was stunned by the kindness of so many people, many of whom she didn't know well at all. She couldn't help but think how different things would be if she were still in New York. She might have received flowers from her colleagues, but they would have been purchased by their secretaries, and she couldn't think of one person who would have cared enough to come and see her. Well, maybe Jamie. And Wallace Finn. But it would have been nothing like this outpouring of love and friendship.

For the first time since Emily had left with the Kimballs, Grace felt like smiling.

The doctor pronounced her okay to go home the following morning, but he warned her she would have to take it easy. "That wound could reopen if you're not careful," he said.

Meg came to get her, saying her mother and aunt were already at her house.

For the next week, Grace continued to have a steady stream of visitors who brought her meals and gifts or simply came to talk and tell her how glad they were that she'd survived. One of those visitors was one of the EMTs who had treated her at the scene of the shooting.

Jeff Harrison was tall, young and very good-looking, with a great smile, thick blond hair and unusual gray eyes. Grace figured he was in his early thirties. He stayed for more than an hour, asking her all kinds of questions about herself. When she asked why he was so interested, he admitted she was his first gunshot patient.

Almost shyly, before he left, he asked her if he could take her out for pizza and beer sometime, saying he really admired her and the work she was doing.

Grace knew he was too young for her, but there was

something about him she found very appealing. Maybe she *would* go out with him, she thought. It was only then she realized she wasn't going back to New York.

How could she leave when she had so many wonderful people here who cared about her? So many women and children who needed her? She was humbled and deeply touched by their friendship and concern. When she'd lost Emily, she'd believed she'd given up her career and her life in New York for nothing.

But now she realized that what she had gained in Seacrest was ten times more valuable than what she had left behind in New York. She would always love and miss Emily and wish she could have kept her, but the short period of time she did have Emily had enriched her life and opened it to possibilities she'd never have dreamed of pursuing before.

And Emily wasn't completely out of her life. Grace could send cards, letters, gifts. She could visit. She was no longer shackled by a relentless work schedule and killer caseload. She had a different life now, a better life. And when Emily got older, she could come to Florida. After all, her grandmother lived here, too.

As Grace stood at the door and waved goodbye to Jeff, her heart felt so full, and she finally saw that if she would just open herself to it, there was no telling what the next phase of her life might bring.

I owe my sister more than I can ever repay.
—*From an entry in Grace Campisi's journal*

EPILOGUE

Two years later…

"Grace, will you please sit down?"

Grace made a face at Craig. "I can't. I'm too nervous. What if—?" She couldn't finish the thought. Couldn't stand to think how she would feel if, for some reason, the judge didn't grant their petition.

He rose and walked to where she stood. Putting his arms around her, Craig kissed her softly. "Everything is going to be fine, sweetheart. Trust me on this."

"Oh, you'd say that even if you thought it wasn't," Grace said. But there was no sting in the comment, for she knew Craig's assurances came from love and not from any lawyerly platitudes. She smiled up at him, thinking how glad she was that he had finally worn down her defenses. Then, as she did dozens of times each day, she glanced down at the beautiful diamond wedding band that adorned her left ring finger. A shaft of sunlight coming through the fourth-floor window of the county courthouse fired the stones with brilliant color.

She and Craig had just returned from a glorious three-week honeymoon in Italy. And now they were waiting to hear Judge Richards' verdict on their petition to adopt the two young children Grace had been fostering for the past year.

Thinking about Ethan and Brook, Grace's heart seized up with a mixture of fear, love and hope. They were such wonderful kids, and they'd had such a rough time. Five-year-old Ethan and four-year-old Brook had captured her heart almost from the first moment she'd laid eyes on them—two scared little kids whose mother had collapsed on the street, then died ten days later.

Just then, the door to the judge's chambers opened and the bailiff said, "Judge Richards will see you now."

Grace slipped her hand into Craig's and he squeezed it.

Judge Richards looked up from her desk as they walked into her chambers. She invited them to sit down. Grace looked around, but the children were not there.

"I asked Abbie to take the children into the other room so we could talk privately," the Judge said.

Grace's eyes met Craig's. Was that a good sign?

He smiled at her.

Grace took a deep breath.

"Let me reassure you immediately," Judge Richards said. "I'm going to grant your petition."

Grace couldn't prevent the "oh" that escaped her in a relieved gasp.

Judge Richards smiled. "Both of the children love you very much," she said. "That was obvious from our talk. And," she added, turning her gaze to Craig, "they seem to love you, too, Mr. Mancuso. I feel confident that they'll have a good home with the two of you."

The judge talked to them for another fifteen minutes, told them when the official papers would be ready for their signatures, then called for the bailiff to bring the children back to her chambers.

When the two tow headed youngsters entered the room, Brook immediately broke away from her brother and raced toward Grace. Grace, smiling through her tears, picked up the sturdy little girl and put her on her lap. Ethan, shier and quieter than bubbly Brook, walked over to Craig, who put his arm around the boy. His eyes met Grace's. In them, she saw the same mixture of emotions she felt.

They smiled at each other.

"Good luck," Judge Richards said. She smiled, too.

"Thank you," Grace whispered. She hugged Brook tighter. *I am so blessed,* she thought.

As the new family walked out of the courthouse, Grace said, "Guess what? Aunt Perry is bringing Emily to visit us in two weeks."

"She *is?*" piped Brook. Delight shone in her eyes.

"Is Emily our cousin now?" Ethan asked.

Grace grinned. "She is. And Grandma Stella is your grandmother now and Aunt Mutt is your aunt, too."

"Our *great*-aunt," Ethan said.

Craig chuckled. "Mr. Literal has spoken."

"Yes," Grace agreed. "Your great-aunt."

"And now you're our *Mom*," Brook said. She turned her enchanting smile to Craig. "And *you're* our Dad."

"Exactly right, kiddo," Craig said, dropping a kiss on the top of her head.

Exactly right, thought Grace, whose heart was so full, she was afraid it might burst. *My cup runneth over....*

"Let's go home," Craig said, his eyes once more meeting Grace's. *I love you*, he mouthed.

"Ditto," Grace said.

*Experience entertaining women's fiction
about rediscovery and reconnection—warm,
compelling stories that are relevant
for every woman who has wondered
"What's next?" in their lives.
After all, there's the life you planned.
And there's what comes next.*

*Turn the page for a sneak preview
of a new book from Harlequin NEXT.*

CONFESSIONS OF A NOT-SO-DEAD LIBIDO
by Peggy Webb

*On sale November 2006,
wherever books are sold.*

My husband could see beauty in a mud puddle. Literally. "Look at that, Louise," he'd say after a heavy spring rain. "Have you ever seen so many amazing colors in mud?"

I'd look and see nothing except brown, but he'd pick up a stick and swirl the mud till the colors of the earth emerged, and all of a sudden I'd see the world through his eyes—extraordinary instead of mundane.

Roy was my mirror to life. Four years ago when he died, it cracked wide open, and I've been living a smashed-up, sleepwalking life ever since.

If he were here on this balmy August night I'd be sailing with him instead of baking cheese straws in preparation for Tuesday-night quilting club with Patsy. I'd be striving for sex appeal in Bermuda shorts and bare-toed sandals instead of opting for comfort in walking shoes and a twill skirt with enough elastic around the waist to make allowances for two helpings of lemon-cream pie.

Not that I mind Patsy. Just the opposite. I love her. She's the only person besides Roy who creates wonder wherever she goes. (She creates mayhem, too, but we won't get into that.) She's my mirror now, as well as my compass.

Of course, I have my daughter, Diana, but I refuse to be the kind of mother who defines herself through her children. Besides, she has her own life now, a husband and a baby on the way.

I slide the last cheese straws into the oven and then go into my office and open e-mail.

From: "Miss Sass" <patsyleslie@hotmail.com>
To: "The Lady" <louisejernigan@yahoo.com>
Sent: Tuesday, August 15, 6:00 PM
Subject: Dangerous Tonight
Hey Lady,
I'm feeling dangerous tonight. Hot to trot, if you know what I mean. Or can you even remember? ☺ Look out, bridge club, here I come. I'm liable to end up dancing on the tables instead of bidding three spades. Whose turn is it to drive, anyhow? Mine or thine?
XOXOX
Patsy
P.S. Lord, how did we end up in a club with no men?

This e-mail is typical "Patsy." She's the only person I know who makes me laugh all the time. I guess that's why I e-mail her about ten times a day. She lives right next door, but e-mail satisfies my urge to be instantly and constantly in touch with her without having to interrupt the

flow of my life. Sometimes we even save the good stuff for
e-mail.

From: "The Lady" <louisejernigan@yahoo.com>
To: "Miss Sass" <patsyleslie@hotmail.com>
Sent: Tuesday, August 15, 6:10 PM
Subject: Re: Dangerous Tonight
So, what else is new, Miss Sass? You're always danger-
ous. If you had a weapon, you'd be lethal. ☺
Hugs,
Louise
P.S. What's this about men? I thought you said your
libido was dead?

I press Send then wait. Her reply is almost instantaneous.

From: "Miss Sass" <patsyleslie@hotmail.com>
To: "The Lady" <louisejernigan@yahoo.com>
Sent: Tuesday, August 15, 6:12 PM
Subject: Re: Dangerous Tonight
Ha! If I had a *brain* I'd be lethal.
And I said my libido was in hibernation, not DEAD!
Jeez, Louise!!!!!
P

Patsy loves to have the last word, so I shut off my
computer.

*****

*Want to find out what happens to their friendship
when Patsy and Louise both find the perfect man?*

Don't miss
CONFESSIONS OF A NOT-SO-DEAD LIBIDO
by Peggy Webb,

*coming to Harlequin NEXT
in November 2006.*

Solitary confinement never looked so good!

Instant motherhood felt a lot like being under house arrest, until somewhere between dealing with a burned bake-sale project, PTA meetings and preteen dating, Kate realized she'd never felt so free.

Motherhood Without Parole

by Tanya Michaels

HARLEQUIN®
Next™

HN65

Available November 2006
TheNextNovel.com

True Confessions
of the
Stratford Park PTA

by Nancy Robards
Thompson

The journey of four women through midlife;
man trouble; and their children's middle
school hormones—as they find their place
in this world...

Available October 2006
TheNextNovel.com

Some secrets are meant to be shared.

For a group of friends, this summer will
be remembered forever as the year when
Rose's family became complete, Doris
became the woman she was always meant
to be and Mercedes finally found her man.
It's never too late to give the rest of the town
something to talk about.

The Gossip Queens

by Kate Austin

REQUEST YOUR FREE BOOKS!

2 FREE NOVELS PLUS 2 FREE GIFTS!

There's the life you planned. And there's what comes next.

If only Harvey the Wonder Dog could dig up the dirt on her ex!

The last person she expected to see at her husband's funeral was his other wife! Penny can't bring herself to hate his "wife" or toss his amazing piano-playing dog out on his rump. But thanks to her ex's legacy and Harvey's "amazing" trainer, Penny's ready to run with whatever curveball life throws at her!

The Other Wife

by Shirley Jump

HN68

Available November 2006
TheNextNovel.com

A stunning novel of love and renewal...

Everyone knows sisters like the Sams girls—
three women trying their best to be good
daughters, mothers and wives. Then in one
cataclysmic moment everything changes...
and the sisters have to uncover every shrouded
secret and risk lifetime bonds to ensure the
survival of all they love.

Graceland

by Lynne Hugo